GORE GLEN

CULLEN & BAIN 4

ED JAMES

OTHER BOOKS BY ED JAMES

SCOTT CULLEN MYSTERIES SERIES

1. GHOST IN THE MACHINE
2. DEVIL IN THE DETAIL
3. FIRE IN THE BLOOD
4. STAB IN THE DARK
5. COPS & ROBBERS
6. LIARS & THIEVES
7. COWBOYS & INDIANS
8. HEROES & VILLAINS

CULLEN & BAIN SERIES

1. CITY OF THE DEAD
2. WORLD'S END
3. HELL'S KITCHEN
4. GORE GLEN

CRAIG HUNTER SERIES

1. MISSING
2. HUNTED
3. THE BLACK ISLE

DS VICKY DODDS

1. TOOTH & CLAW
2. FLESH & BLOOD
3. SKIN & BONE (May 2021)

DI SIMON FENCHURCH SERIES

1. THE HOPE THAT KILLS

PROLOGUE

'The Scottish School Minister, Dr Isobel Geddes, had this to say.'

'I'm afraid that it's still far too early in the lockdown timeline to be able to project a return to school. That said, we are working with all stakeholders to—'

Isobel Geddes hit the stereo's power button. Her car's headlights cut through the gloom, the only vehicle on the road, but she still felt like she was being followed.

And hearing herself speaking on the radio like that?

None of the training the party had forced on her over the years could make her not *hate* her voice. Hearing herself speaking hauled her back to standing in front of a class, reading from a book in her dull monotone, jerking her way through the paragraph like a robot. While all the other kids laughed and whispered and pointed. And Isobel stopped, just standing there, frozen, while the laughter became louder, and the teacher got more and more impatient with her, to the point of anger.

Some things stayed with you all your life.

While she couldn't do anything to change her past, Isobel could help other kids going through similar trauma.

Up ahead, the lights of Stow glowed against the darkening sky, the hills on either side of the road overpowering the low sun. On most Friday evenings, this road would be filled with tourists heading north from England, or people like her returning to their weekend homes.

Isobel realised she was grinding her teeth again, digging the top molars into the bottom. Becoming a bad habit, and she had inside knowledge on the prospect of having no access to dental care for a long time.

It came down to hating being slave to the fear. No, she had learned to conquer it long ago. But still, her voice... That was hard to change.

She slowed as she entered the village, quiet and dark as if it was during the Blitz, just the streetlights ruining the illusion. What the country was going through was nowhere near as severe as back then, but Isobel received all the latest reports and knew how bad it really was. The projections of cases, of deaths, of economic losses, of suicides, of excess deaths, and what was within her own remit: the long-term psychological trauma to children because they were being homeschooled by parents struggling with a world falling apart while trying to do their own jobs.

It was a lot to deal with. A glass of red wine, a gin and tonic, a beer, or a whisky would only go so far. And soon the drinking would become a habit, compounding the misery.

The lights at the crossroad were red, so Isobel played that game of trying to take it as slow as she could, and then sneak through just as it hit green, not having to stop.

But her timing was off. Green came when she was twenty metres away.

Then again, there was no queue of stalled cars ahead of her, so she eased through.

A flash of blue lights up ahead, dancing off the old ruined bridge, then the blast of siren caught up.

Police.

She shouldn't be out, and yet here she was, driving home. Unable to do anything else, really.

They'd stop her, ask where she was going, what she was doing, see that she was miles from her regular home in Edinburgh. Maybe someone in the party would be able to hold some sway and delay a charge, but maybe not. And maybe it would leak to the press. Her career would be over. Worse, she wouldn't be able to help kids like her younger self, struggling with a school system that wasn't working for them.

Relief surged in her gut as an ambulance powered past. Some poor unfortunate up in Heriot or Fountainhall maybe, waiting to be collected before heading down to the Borders General. Not many cases down here at all, and things were still almost normal.

She slowed as she approached her turning and reached down to press her gate key, but nothing happened.

Fantastic.

Isobel opened her door and stepped out into the cool evening air. The clicker thing didn't work, so she had to walk over and press the button.

The gate whirred as it opened wide.

Isobel needed to get that fixed, but who knew when it would be safe for the man to come out? She looked up and down the main street through the village, but there was nobody about, not even a late dog walker getting their government-sanctioned exercise after putting the kids to bed.

She got back in the car and put it in gear, but didn't drive through.

No, there was somebody about, parked between two cones of light, the exhaust pluming in the darkness. An old Mondeo, blue and battered like it had been thrashed around the B-roads by an idiot. Just like her ex-husband's car.

Sneaky little worm. Staking out their old home, waiting for her to return when she should be thirty miles north. What was he going to spring on her now? Pathetic.

The car shot off, the driver tugging on his seatbelt as he sped away towards Edinburgh.

It wasn't Peter. She could see that. But she had absolutely no idea who it was.

A lot of people would want to spy on her, the Scottish Minister for Schools. She should be in Edinburgh, self-isolating in her tiny flat, but here she was down in the Borders, at a second home. Very few voters would have sympathy for her privileged position, even though she worked long hours, trying to build a strategy for the safe return of the nation's children and teachers, while everything else shifted and changed beneath her feet.

No, she needed the release of her weekends to even begin to cope with the stress weighing her down constantly.

Well. Assuming it was malicious, and not some eerie coincidence, there was nothing she could do, other than lie. Some nonsense about getting a warning that there was an issue with the house that could've caused a fire, and maybe that her cleaner was ill and couldn't attend. Historic old manse house, been here as long as there's been a village. She needed to save it, didn't want to trouble the police.

Something like that. People would understand. And the party would support her. Tell the lie loudly enough and stick to your guns, then people stop caring and move on to the next story. She had enough goodwill built up to call in enough favours.

Isobel drove on through the gates and—*mercy*—the clicker worked this time. Maybe she didn't need to get the man out after all.

She edged into the drive and parked outside her home, the big old pile in the heart of the village. Home it was. All hers. She got out and sucked in the fresh air. The lights of the locked-down houses glowed around her, but the place was deadly silent, save for the whisper of the Gala Water winding through the village. Twenty-five miles from the parliament, but it felt like a thousand.

Calmness surrounded her, that knot in the top of her spine easing off that little bit.

She locked her car and walked over to the side door. Time was, this would've been for servants, but now it was the main way in. Still had the original key, a huge black thing that slid in and clicked with a satisfying sound. The sheer size of the thing was enough security.

Isobel stepped into the house and felt the reassuring warmth crawl up her bare arms. It might be old, but having a remote trigger for the central heating was sheer bliss at a time like this. She dumped her briefcase under the coat rack.

A strong arm wrapped around her throat. Fingers covered her mouth.

Isobel tried to fight, to bite, to chew, to claw, to elbow, but he was far too strong for her. 'Stop!' Her legs went out from under her, and she was pushed to the floor. 'Let me go!'

Big meaty hands grabbed her hair and pressed her cheeks against the cold flagstones. 'You're in deep trouble, Isobel.'

1

The screaming clawed at Cullen's ears, almost deafening. Then a flailing hand caught him in the balls and he went down to his knees, stars flashing across his vision. The living room seemed to swim around him. The deep pain stung, climbing up into his stomach and down his thighs, forcing him to shut his eyes.

Every time he caught a blow down there, it took him back to the playground, to that little shite David Green punching him quicker than he could block. Every bloody day. Sometimes two or three times.

A hand gripped his shoulder and Cullen tensed, instincts readying him for what was coming next.

'I'm sorry, Uncle Scott.'

Cullen opened his eyes and focused on Declan standing there, not even at head height when Cullen was slumped on his knees. So small, and yet those wild swings of his could be deadly. 'One of those things, Dec.' He messed up the wee sod's spiked hair and got a slimy handful of damp gel for his trouble.

Evie knelt down next to Cullen, her plaited hair hanging over her left shoulder. Her cute smile filled that heart-shaped face, with the hidden menace of this being something she'd repeat again and again. 'Declan, why don't you go and find your brother?'

'Okay, Auntie Yvonne.' And Declan shot off, a blur of energy hunting around the poky flat.

The ball ache had lessened, so Cullen huffed in a breath and stood up. 'You have no idea how much this hurts.'

Evie shook her head. 'Don't even think about joking that it's worse than childbirth.'

'Never crossed my mind.' Cullen sat back on the sofa and got a fresh throb of ball pain. 'But it bloody hurts.'

'Aw, diddums.' Evie rubbed her finger over his lips. 'Seriously, though, are you okay?'

'I'm fine. That kid's got his mum's speed.'

Evie arched her eyebrow. 'And his old man's anger issues.'

Cullen had to shut his eyes again. 'Don't.'

'Sorry, Scott, I shouldn't have.' Evie sat next to him, arms folded. 'Not even to joke about it.'

Cullen looked around the room. Over three years since the kids had lost their father. 'I wish I could've saved him.'

'Scott, I was there, remember? There's no way anyone could've saved him.' She touched his thigh, gentle and soft. 'And you did the best you could. Imagine if you and Methven hadn't fudged it so Angela got her widow's pension?'

She was right. There were lines you could cross, lines you shouldn't, and lines you just bloody had to. Grey areas, murky truths, but Cullen knew that they had done the right thing. Angela Caldwell and her kids were the victims of what happened, and they needed to be protected.

And here they were, Cullen and Evie, spending their Monday morning babysitting for Angela as she sat her sergeant's exams. On the long road to recovery, to rebuilding a life, to building a new one, a future for her sons.

But Cullen couldn't help but feel like he was on trial, with Evie watching his every move with the kids, trying to suss out if he was the right man to have kids with. She was barely eight months older than him, both late thirties now, and time was catching up with them. Now or never, really.

Cullen felt that tickling in his throat, then his chest. That horrific cough that still lingered after almost two months. Not many people he knew had caught Covid-19, but those that did, they knew all about it. That feeling like someone was sitting on your chest all day, and you couldn't punch *them* in the balls either. Touch and go too, a few hours in April where he felt like he needed to go to hospital. But it broke like a sea storm, and he felt a lot better. Didn't stop this constant cough, though. It rattled through him, like the virus was back in his body and he no longer had the antibodies to fight it off.

He slumped back in the sofa and let his breathing recover a bit. A notification flashed up on his phone, resting on the side table. A new podcast episode. And he caught the words "The Secret Rozzer". And he couldn't do anything but groan.

'What?'

He picked up his phone and looked over at Evie. 'There's another episode of that podcast.'

'Seriously?'

'Seriously.' Cullen couldn't resist any longer, so tapped the notification. It took him into the app, but didn't start playing. He read the description aloud: 'This week on the Secret Rozzer, our intrepid ex-cop talks about his ex-boss's favouritism, usually in favour of officers of the female persuasion. Levelling the playing field? Or setting up future favours of a sexual nature? We want our army of rozzers to decide!' He tossed his phone onto the table again, hard enough that he could've cracked the screen. 'This is absolute bollocks. I can't—'

'What did your lawyer say?'

Cullen folded his arms and sighed. 'Like I told you... These might be my antics, even though they're slightly fictionalised, but if I did anything about it, I'd likely incur the Streisand Effect.'

Evie grinned, her cheek dimpling. 'You mean, when you try to stamp it out, you just draw attention to it?'

'Right. And it'd mean admitting that I did these things.'

'There's nothing wrong with promoting female officers, Scott. It's good how your three sergeants are female. Besides, six of your eight constables are male.'

Cullen couldn't look at her. 'But one of them was one I demoted a couple of months ago.'

'And he's a constable who you know does a podcast. A

constable who you know hates your guts, who's tried to get you fired on so many occasions.'

'I *know* it's Bain doing it, I just can't prove it.' Cullen hit play and the distorted voice spoke out of his phone's speakers.

'Welcome to the Secret Rozzer, boys and girls. If you sit nicely, then we'll begin.' Definitely male, but deeper than natural and weird phasing effects on it, enough to mask it, but not enough to make it unlistenable. And no traces of an accent, either. There was a robotic rhythm to it, like it could be one of those AI things. 'My old boss, let's call him Jock, shall we? Because he is Scott ... ish. And he's from a wee town up in Aberdeenshire, between Buckie and Banff.'

'See what I mean? That just about names me! Scott and Cullen. I mean...' Cullen hit the pause button.

'Right. But there's nothing in it, is there?'

'Of course there's not.'

'It's just that you've got a bit of previous with long-term relationships with female sergeants.'

'Sadly, I'm not gay so that precludes me from relationships with male ones.'

'Sadly?'

'You know what I mean, Evie. And you don't believe me?'

'Scott, I'm a cop. My job is to ask enough questions and assess the answers so that I can truly believe people.'

'Fair.' Cullen stared at the phone, wanting to smash it into a thousand pieces. But the podcast wasn't there, it was in the cloud, wherever that was, and distributed to hundreds, maybe thousands of phones just like his. People starting to listen to his antics, even though this one was absolute dogshit.

Then his phone rang.

Methven calling...

'The bloody boss.'

'Scott, don't you dare.'

'I'm not planning on answering it.' Cullen shut off the ringer and let it go to voicemail all on its own. He leaned in and wrapped his arm around Evie.

Footsteps thundered up and down the stairs.

And the phone rang again. Still Methven.

Cullen looked at Evie. 'This'll be about that podcast. Maybe I should get it.'

'You think?'

Cullen answered. 'Good morning, sir.'

Methven grumbled something unintelligible.

'Sorry, sir, I didn't catch that. If this is about the podcast, then—'

'What sodding podcast?'

Cullen did everything but look at Evie. 'The Secret Rozzer, sir.'

Methven sighed. 'I'd completely forgotten about that. Why? Have you found out who's behind it?'

'No, sir.'

'Hmm.'

'Never mind.' Cullen caught himself biting his thumbnail. 'What's up?'

'I'm afraid I'm having to cancel your leave, Inspector.'

Evie got up, hands on hips.

'Can't DS Jain cover the—'

'This isn't about that, no. Besides, while she is back on duty, her medical advice is that she's still under instructions to self-isolate, and is only on back-office duties. So, I'm really short-staffed, Scott. Please.'

'Sir, I'm not sure I can come in.'

'Scott, are you telling me you can't work?'

'Eh?'

'Are you under the influence?'

'Eh? Of course not, no. We're looking after Angela Caldwell's kids while—'

'I need you to come in. Please, Scott.'

Cullen fell back into the sofa.

Evie turned round to look at him, eyes narrowed. As much as this cut both ways, Cullen hated seeing the disappointment of a lost day in her eyes. Worse, having to manage the sons of Satan on her own.

'Sir, if there's any way that—'

'No, Scott, there's not. In fact, given it's two cases we're dealing with here, to help us cope, I've had to beg, borrow and steal. DS Luke Shepherd is just returning to DI Davenport's team from a stint in Professional Standards and Ethics, so doesn't have an active caseload.'

Shepherd. Big bear of a man who Cullen had worked with back in the day, when he was a total arsehole, rather than just the partial one he was now. 'Right. I know Luke.'

'Is he good?'

'In a way. Surprised he's still a DS.'

'Well, DS Shepherd comes highly recommended, but those recommendations are fairly often tainted. Besides, one of the cases is on his old patch. A missing persons from the Parliament.'

Cullen locked eyes with Evie, but there just wasn't any way he was getting out of this. She saw that too, staring up at the ceiling. 'Okay, sir. We're out in Garleton just now, so I'll be about half an hour getting in.'

'No, Scott, I need you to take charge of a case in Midlothian. A dead body in Gore Glen. I'll text you the details.' A click and Methven was gone.

Cullen got up and stuffed his phone into his pocket. 'Take it you heard that?'

'Enough of it.' Evie looked at him. 'Why is it that bosses have to *insist* on things?'

'Don't they just... It's... Look, I'm really sorry about this.'

'I know you are, Scott.' She pecked him on the cheek. 'Just make sure Angela comes here right after her exams, okay?'

2

Tell you, this whole nonsense about social distancing is getting my goat already.

One of the great pleasures of the day is doing a jobbie with the day's paper. All the salacious gossip up front, then Dear Deirdre or her many rivals on the way through, just depends on which paper is the cheapest, then finish off with seeing whatever the Rangers are up to now. Save the best for last.

But no. The powers that be have decided that you can only have one dump station in the St Leonard's Gents, even though the doors are shut. Doubt that the lassies have to put up with this.

And some boy's already in there, grunting and groaning as he pushes out his morning load.

I scone my left foot—back in my playing days, some have described it as a "cultured left foot", some even as "a wand of a left foot"—off the door. 'Have some All Bran, pal.' Then I scoot over to the urinals and unfurl Wee Brian, then piss away, with the paper tucked under my arm.

Ah, bliss.

The main door clatters open and footsteps thump across the tiles towards us.

Years of service make us flinch in situations like this, but it's the bogs in a cop shop, who's going to attack Brian Bain? Way too many candidates. Besides, I'm mid-flow here.

No social distancing at the urinals, is there? Elbow to elbow with this lunatic. 'Just made it.' English accent. And his piss is a big gush, compared to my steady trickle.

A cheeky wee glance down at the boy's plonker and, bloody hell, there is one serious ding-dong down there. At least three of mine.

Christ!

I nudge him a wee bit with my elbow. 'Well, pal, if you've just made it, you fancy making me one as well?'

And I clock the boy's face. It's none other than Simon Buxton, Cullen's latest bum chum. Designer stubble all over his puss, and those new false teeth that make his mouth look all funny. And the boy is blushing, likes. Not that he's paying much attention. Christ, it's like a stallion down there, and not just in length and girth. The sheer blast coming from that thing!

'Only joking, Budgie.' I shake off Wee Brian—never a truer name, is there?—and pat the boy's arm. 'But you're more like an eagle, though, or an albatross. Christ, imagine that thing tied around your neck!'

'Would you shut up?' He's still pissing, but he's pissed off at me.

'Come on, Simon, that's something you should be shouting about from the rooftops!'

The dump-station door opens and none other than Craig Hunter, Cullen's *last* bum chum waltzes out and heads over to the sinks. Boy is big too, but not downstairs. Everywhere else, mind. Muscles in places where I've not—

Better stop thinking about muscles going in places, eh?

Cullen's OG bum chum, as the hip hop boys would say. Original Gangsta.

I leave Buxton, *still* pissing, and join Hunter at the sinks. He towers over us. Hate standing next to him, but not so much at the urinal. 'Craig, have you seen the size of that thing Budgie's packing?'

Hunter just raises his eyebrows at us. 'Brian...' And he sighs. Sighs. Cheeky sod. 'What's that supposed to mean?'

'You and spying on other cop's todgers go together like white on rice.'

That makes us frown as I lather up my wrists. 'What about brown rice? Or that wild stuff?'

'You know the saying, right?'

'American, aye. Heard it a load in the States in March, just doesn't make sense.' I catch sight of Buxton shaking off, and it's like Indiana Jones with his bullwhip! 'What if you add turmeric to white rice while you're cooking? That makes it go all yellow, right?'

Hunter dries his hands on his breeks. 'Just stop looking at cocks, okay?'

Cheeky sod. Like he's one to talk. Saw both inches of his, once. Poor Chantal, know what I'm saying?

Buxton is coming this way and, Christ, all I can think of is that monster. He must tuck in because his trousers are tight as, and there's no sign of that hog.

I give the lad a sly wink and follow Hunter out into the corridor.

He's standing there, shaking his head, looking at an even bigger bastard. 'Hadn't heard, no.'

Man alive, it's DS Luke Shepherd. Big bugger, as big as Hunter but naturally massive. Greyer than yours truly, mind. Always one, isn't there? That Borders accent of his, got to laugh at it. The slightly hurdy-gurdy nature of it. Mental.

Shepherd is scowling at Hunter, then at me. 'Why are two of my team together in the toilet?'

Makes us frown, likes. '*Your* team?'

'Aye. Orders from DCI Methven. I'm told I'm leading you two and a DC Simon Buxton.'

I nod back at the toilet door. 'There's a lot you can get your hands around there.' I ignore Hunter's scowl and hold my hand out to Shepherd. 'Been a while, Luke.'

'I'd say too long, but eternity wouldn't be enough.' He's got that cheeky git look in his eyes, that's for sure. He waves my paw away. 'One, we don't shake hands anymore. Two, I doubt you've learnt to wash after toileting.'

'Charming as ever, Luke-y boy.'

'Brian, I heard about your recent demotion. Must be painful.'

'Aye. Even the boy who cleans the bogs outranks me.'

'And you don't seem to mind?'

I just shrug. All you can do, eh? 'You can have the extra five grand a year, Luke, but I'll keep the overtime and the complete lack of stress. Besides, I wouldn't want to be responsible for an arsehole like me.'

Shepherd stands there, fuming. Trouble with boys like him, Cullen and Hunter is they think they're God's gift to policing, but they're more like tills in shops, absolutely rammed with buttons I can press. 'So—'

The door opens again and Buxton wanders out. Christ, I can't help but stare at the lack of a bulge in his trousers. That'll haunt my dreams, I tell you!

Shepherd looks like he's keeched himself. 'Simon, were you in there too?'

'Eh, yeah?' Buxton's frowning, like he's missed the joke or we're all talking about the albatross downstairs. 'What's up?'

'In here.' Shepherd opens the meeting-room door and leads in. 'Listen to me, you bunch of idiots.' He tries to draw us together. Social distancing? Mask or no mask, there is no chance I am getting into a huddle with these deviants, so I step away. Not that Shepherd seems to notice. 'I've just spent three years in Professional Standards and Ethics.'

The Complaints. Bad boys and girls.

I shake my head at him. 'You get yourself involved in any Internal Affairs, Luke?'

'I've half a mind to take you into the toilet and flush your head in the pan. But I think you'd enjoy it, wouldn't you?'

Prick.

Shepherd knows he's not getting anything sensible from us, so he focuses his attentions on Hunter and Budgie. Little and Large, eh? 'That means I spent three years investigating bent cops.'

I give them all a grin. 'That's a bit homophobic, isn't it?'

'Not homosexual, Brian. Corrupt. Dodgy. And an established pattern of corrupt officers involves meeting in places where they can't be surveilled. Toilets are perfect, no cameras or sound recordings anywhere. So when I see all three of you meeting in there?'

'Just so happened to be in there, Luke. Craig was having a dump, Simon was... Well, he was running late, wasn't he? It's always good to have a wee pish before the briefing, you know? Sometimes they drag on and on, and you don't want any jiggling legs in there, do you?'

Shepherd scowls, but he's not going to delve any more. 'Right, the reason I'm speaking to you is that I'll be taking over from Lauren Reid while Chantal Jain's off.'

I glance at Hunter, Chantal's current beau, then back at Shepherd. 'She okay?'

'She's fine. Back-office duties. Lauren's covering Chantal's team, so you're stuck with me.'

'Eh, where's Elvis?'

'That's another matter entirely.' Shepherd doesn't even bat an eyelid. 'Okay, so I've caught a Missing Persons case down at Holyrood.'

'In Dumbiedykes?'

'Nope. The parliament. And it's a VIP, hence us getting involved.'

I rub my hands together. 'Tell me more.'

Shepherd gives us a withering look. 'Unless anyone needs to go to the toilet again, then I suggest we get on with our jobs? Me and Simon will head down to Holyrood. Craig, can you babysit Brian to an address in Portobello?'

'Grew up in Porty.' Hunter looks less impressed with that than I do. 'And Brian here never grew up.'

3

Cullen eased down the backroad running in from Gorebridge, bumping over a railway bridge, then it did a dogleg and slipped under a railway bridge, but Cullen had no idea if it was the same bridge, or if it was still in service on the Borders Railway, but he thought the tracks were closer to the town. He drove over another bridge, this time over the river, presumably one of the Esks, but whether it was south or north, well, same as with the bridge, he just didn't know.

What he did know was that the Edinburgh Crime Scene Investigators were out, and in force too. The silly sods had blocked off yet another bridge over the river, but the car park was clear, so he double-parked behind a Jag. He opened his door and stepped out onto the muddy road.

Cullen was sure he had only been to Gore Glen once before, a stormy relationship ago, and couldn't recall much about it. An open gate leading into the glen, guarded by a pair of absolutely stacked male uniforms, like a pair of gargoyles with bulging biceps.

'DI Cullen.' He showed them his warrant card, but they were determined to both get a look at it. Another path climbed the hill, wooden planks acting as steps. And no sign of any of his team.

'On you go, sir.' The uniform on the left nodded him

through with the casual look of a nightclub bouncer, now on to searching the congregating faces piling out of a minivan.

At least it was dry and the path was clear, so Cullen walked on. Old trees ran overhead, beech and oak in the main.

Some CSIs were busy cataloguing footprints, and they guided Cullen off the mud onto a patch of grass. Way too many prints by the looks of it. He knew that work wouldn't likely come to anything, but sometimes you had to try.

Cullen walked on, the path leading him through a canopy of beech, starting to turn from buds to leaves, but not quite making it, with the bare earth criss-crossed by a network of exposed roots.

Still no sign of any of his team. This was getting embarrassing.

He got out his phone to call Lauren.

Answered straight away. 'Scott, where are you?'

The river bubbled away below, with a brick building that had "teen drinking den" written all over it. Actually, it had RFC and Gore Young Team written all over it. 'Thinking of asking you the same question.'

'Well, we're here. And you're not?'

Cullen looked back at the car park, but couldn't see any red hair. 'What can you see?'

'An empty car park?'

'And that doesn't surprise you? Shouldn't you see at least one squad car?'

'Right, but there is one.'

'And they're guarding that entrance for us.' Cullen sighed. 'Left, then left, then left again. And if you miss the first left, use the roundabout.'

'Five minutes.' And she was gone.

~

THE PATH SPLIT, though a uniform directed Cullen down a narrow strip lined with bramble bushes with deer fences on the other side, marking out a pasture leading up to a slight hill. He managed to navigate it without tearing his suit too badly, and came to a slight decline, curving round to a bridge over the river.

And this was where the party was.

A uniform blocked access to the bottom of the hill, crime scene tape doing half the job for him.

Cullen walked up and filled out the form.

'Scott?'

He turned around and saw DS Lauren Reid jogging to catch up, so he added her name to the catalogue and returned it.

She stood there, panting hard, lips as tightly wound as her hair. And always shivering, even after jogging.

'You okay?'

A frown danced across her forehead. 'I'm fine. Why?'

'You've got a face like a wet weekend in Arbroath.'

She rolled her eyes. 'Scott, managing someone isn't—'

'Lauren, if this is about you being shunted over to manage Elvis and Eva Law, then I can only apologise.'

Her nostrils flared slightly. Enough to confirm that he was on the money. She didn't say anything, though.

Cullen walked over to the inner crime scene, through the throng of CSIs. 'These are crazy times, Lauren. We'll all have to make sacrifices to get through them. I appreciate—'

'What sacrifices are you making, Scott?'

'We've only got eight hours left on our shift, which is about a tenth of the time I'd need to detail it. Besides, I'm not even supposed to be on today. Annual leave cancelled.'

'Oh.' She smiled. 'Sorry. And nobody likes a moaner, I know.'

Cullen returned the smile. 'I'm an Olympic-standard moaner. Should see the training I have to do. Do as I say, not as I do, Lauren. Besides, do you really want *my* reputation? Make sure you learn from my mistakes, and be nice to me when you're my DCI.'

Another broad grin, but she huffed out a deep sigh soon after. 'Scott, it's just... Luke Shepherd? Really?'

'You got previous with him?'

She started rubbing her arms, even though the temperature had cleared twenty. And centigrade too. Cullen wasn't one of those weirdos who used Fahrenheit in summer, Celsius in winter.

'I'll take that as a "yes"?'

'It's nothing, it's just... Be careful with him, Scott.'

'Me and Luke Shepherd go back a long way. Ten years, even. I've got the measure of the man. So don't sweat it.'

'Well, maybe he's changed. Maybe he's got a different role, though. You know how he's just finished a stint in Professional Standards?'

'The Complaints, right.'

'Well, he was investigating my old team.'

'Buchan's boys?'

'And girls.'

'He find anything?'

'Not sure. These investigations take a long time, Scott.' She zipped up her fleece jacket over her suit. 'I'm just warning you, that's all.'

'You mean, what if he's not transitioned out of the Complaints over to the MIT? What if he's actually investigating us?'

She locked eyes with him. 'What if he's investigating *you*, Scott?'

'Me?'

'The Secret Rozzer?' She scuttled off across the road towards the inner crime scene.

It made sense. Perfect sense.

Cullen had been given no choice in bringing Shepherd in, just some spurious excuse like Chantal Jain still being on her isolation pattern. Cullen was sure he'd read somewhere that there was no medical reason for people of BAME origin to get Covid worse than anyone else, and God knows his cough was a constant reminder of how bad he'd had it.

And what he knew was that some arsehole—Bain, or someone allied with him—was broadcasting his deepest professional secrets. His most-stupid mistakes, documenting them for the world to hear.

And making him look like an absolute idiot.

Everyone knew.

Someone like Methven, with a long history of clearing out dead wood, of course he would target Cullen to deflect blame from his own shortcomings. He could imagine the back-room deal, where Methven sucked up to the brass in their Specialised Crime Division, and they worked with Professional Standards & Ethics to remove yet another bad apple. Like demoting Bain to DC.

Cullen knew Methven had his back, but he didn't want to risk his own promotion.

Jesus Christ, Cullen was starting to think like Bain.

Lauren was a good officer, but she could be a bit scatter-brained at times. Prone to conspiracy thinking.

No, Cullen just had to get on with the job and focus on the here and now.

DC Eva Law walked over to him, fists clenched. 'Sir.' Barely looked at Cullen before scuttling off towards Lauren. She had that new ice-queen look, expression emotionless, hair dyed silver-grey. Still wouldn't be moved on to another team, despite their history.

Elvis was another matter entirely. Stretching out and yawning the yawn of a new father. His shirt popped out of his trousers, giving a flash of hairy belly. He walked over in Eva's wake, but gave Cullen the nod.

'Paul.' Cullen skipped over to him, matching Elvis's slow pace as they walked. 'Need a word.' He managed to get him to stop by blocking him off.

Elvis scratched at his long sideburns. 'What's up?'

'Another episode of the podcast dropped.'

'Scott, I told you. It's nothing to do with me.'

'Paul, I trust you, okay? I've never outright accused you, but I have asked you to dig into it for me.'

'Scott, since we got back from America, I've been up to my eyeballs in preparing for a baby, then having a baby, then being absolutely shattered from having a new baby screaming the house down every night. You think I've got time to investigate some bloody podcast?'

'I asked — you said you would.'

'And what did your last slave die of?' Elvis shook his head. 'Scott, do you really think it's about you?'

Cullen knew he had to be very careful here. 'I'm worried that the powers that be will think it is about me. There are enough unsubtle hints on there.'

'On iTunes, or whatever Apple call their podcasts thing these days, it's marked as fiction. Are you telling me you really pissed in a sink at a Christmas night out?'

Cullen looked away from him, with that familiar hot tingle climbing his neck. 'Look, Paul, just see what you can find.'

'Fine.'

'Thanks.' Cullen clapped him on the arm. 'And can you see what CCTV you can dig up for this place?'

Elvis looked around the woodland. 'Here?'

'Not *here* here, but the roads to and from it.' Cullen frowned. 'A lot of forestry places have security, right?'

'Don't think this is one of them, Scott.'

'Well, see if it is.' Cullen fixed him with as good a "boss's boss" stare as he could muster. 'And there are a ton of brownie points in you identifying the Secret Rozzer. Don't forget that.'

4

I look over at Hunter in the driving seat. 'You were saying you grew up round here, right?'

'Right.' His fingers tighten on the wheel. Something bad went down, alright. Note to self — abuse that knowledge in future. 'Changed a bit in that time. Bars and cafes and galleries.' Not that any of the ones we're passing are open, mind. 'But a lot of it's the same. The people take a long time to change.' He pulls up at the lights. Streets are deserted, when it's usually rammed. The town hall is basking in the sun, like a bunch of workers at "Taps Aff" o'clock. 'Long time since this place was a town. Now it's just part of Edinburgh.'

The other way, the blue sea stretches all the way over to North Berwick and the law poking up at the sky like my boy when he was wee, desperate for an ice cream. The boozer on the corner is called The Glassblower. Remember when a couple of letters had fallen off the sign and it said "assblower".

'You worked with Shepherd before, right?'

Hunter nods, eyes locked on the traffic. It's coming from the left, but it'll be our turn soon enough. 'Back in St Leonards. Years ago. Me and Scott worked for him.'

'Christ, you've been a DC that long?'

'Twelve years, but in and out of uniform.'

'Why are you still doing this?'

Hunter looks over at us. 'Why are *you* still doing this?'

'Doing what?'

'This job, Brian. It's shite. You hate it, and everyone hates you.'

I grin at him. 'Not everyone.'

'Okay, so everyone except Elvis.'

'Elvis isn't speaking to me anymore, but Craig my friend, it's not going to be for long.'

Hunter sets off onto the junction, waiting his turn to go right. 'Oh?'

I settle back in my seat. 'Aye, I'm just waiting for my inheritance from my old man's death.'

'Sorry about that. I hadn't heard.'

'Three weeks back. Passed away in his sleep, the old bugger. Not even Covid. Just a long time of being a jakey bugger.' Christ, it's actually making me emotional here. 'But he left it all to me in his will. A ton of cash I'd paid him for his old house, the family pile, and the big place in the Highlands.'

Hunter takes the turning when I wouldn't, what with there being a monster bus hurtling towards us. Gets round in one piece, though. 'Aye?'

'Aye. Up past Lairg. Lovely, I tell you. And we're thinking of selling our pile and moving there. Live the life of Riley, sit back and let people like you, Cullen and Luke Shepherd do the donkey work. Let you make a royal arse of doing the donkey work.' I tap him on the arm. 'A royal *ass* of the *donkey* work.'

But Hunter's not smiling as he takes the next left. 'I met your better half in hospital a couple of months ago. She seems nice.'

'Apinya is a goddess, Craig. A goddess. Way better than I deserve. How's your missus?'

Hunter pulls into the street, but there's a Range Rover trying to get through some shonky double-parking. 'We're not married.'

'I know that. But how is wee Chantal?'

'She's got to look after her parents, so she's been told to self-isolate from work and from me. It's been hard on our relationship.'

'Sorry to hear that.'

'Are you.' Statement, not a question. He slaloms round the Range Rover and pulls up outside the address.

Nice place, have to say. Brighton Crescent is Portobello, not even Joppa, the posh bit, but boy is it fancy. Big old Georgian or Victorian or whatever houses. A long terrace of two storey-things, in a crescent like crisps on your plate in a café, tucked in by the coleslaw of the wee park.

Heh, quite like that. Could murder a bag of salt and vinegar just now. Stomach's rumbling and two bacon rolls can only go so far, eh?

I get out and look around the place, but I can't for the life of me see why an MSP would live out here. 'You're absolutely positive that this is the place?'

Hunter's frowning at us. Again. Boy's making a habit of it. 'Why do you think it isn't?'

'Well, Craig, it's just that it's bit of a stretch from here to the parly in Holyrood, isn't it?' I wave off in the direction I think the parliament is in, but all I can see from here is the train line a wee bitty over, hanging above the other houses and some trees. 'Must be ten miles.'

Hunter barks out a laugh. One of those snide ones that doesn't have any humour. He thinks I'm a fanny. 'Ten miles, eh?' He shakes his head. 'Ten miles and you'd be past the zoo, probably the other end of the bypass, you clown.'

'Clown?' I get in his face. 'Who do you think you're calling a clown?'

He just stands there, like he's dealing with a wee laddie. Then he looks down at my feet. 'Those are mighty long shoes there. And make sure your car doesn't fall apart when you start it.'

'Listen, you big bugger, I was a DI for—'

'*Was.* You're a DC again. So why don't you just shut up, quit moaning and get on with doing your job?'

Big bugger has got us. I shove my paws deep into my pockets while he walks over to the house and tries the bell. 'Isobel Geddes is one of the Regional MSPs for South Scotland, right?'

'Schools Minister too.' Still got the printout in my pocket. 'She lives in Edinburgh, though.' Sure enough, this is the address. I give her a whistle. 'Expensive pad this.'

'And then some.' Hunter tries the bell again, then peeks through the blinds. 'Place looks empty.'

And he's right. Not a sight or a sound. 'So an MSP doesn't turn up for work, and we're supposed to look for her?'

'It's that or head down to Gorebridge with Scott and company.' Hunter squats down, with precise control I have to say, and opens the letterbox. 'Police! Ms Geddes! It's the police!' He peeks through, then hauls himself back up. 'Nobody in.'

I rub my hands together, a nice gesture to indicate how I'm taking charge of this situation. Craig here might be able to squat like that, but he's not been a DI. Or a DS. 'You take the neighbours, I'll head across the street. See what's what. Ten minutes, then meet back at the motor.'

'Fine.' Boy looks relieved to be getting away from Yours Truly. Well, the feeling's mutual, pal. 'Okay.' He steps over the low wall to the next door, already onto the next task.

Got him working for me. Priceless.

I check the moby as I cross the road, nothing much of interest except a new episode of that Secret Rozzer podcast. Would love to shake the boy's hand. I put the phone away and take a good look at the three houses opposite. Not necessarily about who has the best view, is it? Sometimes it's who's in or who's twitching their curtains.

BINGO.

I head up the left-most of the three paths and rap on the door. Old-fashioned, good ol' police officer pattern.

Christ, my mask!

I search my pockets for it, and there it is. I snap it on around my lugs and over my mouth, just as the door opens to a crack.

A wisened old wifie's face looks out, that sort of brown skin that my old boy had, God rest his soul. She's got a mask and goggles on herself. No chance she's catching anything from anyone. 'Can I help you, sir?'

'Police, madam.' I hold up my warrant card, and I swear it still stings saying these words, 'DC Brian Bain, madam.'

'You can't come in.'

'Don't need to—'

'I'll die if I catch that Covid.'

'I understand, madam. I lost my father to it just recently.' Stretching the truth a little, but it yields promising results from her, judging by her frown. Can't teach an old dog new tricks, maybe, but this old dog has the best tricks. The *best*. 'Looking to speak to one of your neighbours.'

'Oh?' The door opens wide now. Trick with these types is to tease them with just a wee bit of gossip and mystery. Works wonders.

'Aye, she didn't turn up at work this morning.'

'And she's the Schools Minister, isn't she?' Oh, she's on the ball this one.

'That she is. So you can see why we're looking to find her.'

'Well, I haven't seen Isobel since Friday morning when she left for work.'

'When was this?'

'Just a minute, son.' She disappears back into her house, but the tang of her cigarette smoke cuts through even this mask.

Bliss. Been a long time since I had one. A very long time.

The door opens and she comes back out, clutching a wee brown leather book. Oh ho ho, she's a professional standard curtain twitcher! 'Let me see... Isobel, Isobel, Isobel. Yes, she left at half past five on Friday morning.'

'That's early.'

'I barely sleep.'

'I meant for her.'

'Oh, yes. Well, she cycles in, so I presume it means she cuts through the park and can avoid the traffic. Then she must shower at the parliament, of course, it's quite the cycle. And then she'll have important matters of state to attend to before a full working day.'

Christ, it's like this old wifie has been stalking her down at the parly too! 'So you didn't see her this weekend?'

She snaps the book shut. 'I *never* see her at the weekend.'

'Oh?'

'That's another matter entirely.'

'What do you—'

'I'm sorry, but it's one that I'm afraid I can't help you with.'

I whip out my own notebook and write it all down. 'Okay, that's been massively helpful, Mrs...?'

'Armitage. Mrs Archibald Armitage.' She hands us a card, a little white thing with doilies and all that crud. Church organist by the looks of it. Well, takes all sorts.

'Thank you for your time, Mrs Armitage.'

'Oh, please call me Maureen. Everyone does.' And with a little flash of flirtatiousness, she closes the door.

Okay, so I can see Hunter hanging around by the car, so I need to get this straight in my head first.

He looks up from his own notebook as I approach. 'Get anything?'

'You first.'

'Well, nobody in at either neighbour. But you seem to hit it off with her.'

'All about charming them, Craig.' I tap my notebook. 'Aye, old Maureen there kept a close eye on Isobel Geddes, that's for sure. Along with the whole street. Said she's not been here since Friday morning. But that's not unusual.'

'Oh?'

'Well, this is a dead end here, but it begs a few questions about where she spends her weekends, doesn't it?'

He rasps a hand across his shaved bonce. 'Let's get down to the parliament.'

'Aye, eager to see how much of an arse Shepherd's made of it.'

5

Every time he had to deal with him, Cullen wished that DC Malcolm McKeown would stop smirking like that. Like he knew his innermost thoughts and found them absolutely hysterical, but only wanted him to see that he knew. Or that he wanted him to see that he knew that he knew that he knew.

Christ. Even thinking that melted his brain.

'Good morning, sir.' Medium height and slight build, but with the deep voice of a bear man, McKeown was usually an afterthought in Cullen's world, one of those rows on a spreadsheet that he had to have to make up numbers, but who he delegated to Lauren and Chantal to manage. Couldn't even remember which one was in charge of him.

Christ, Cullen didn't know what he'd become with his new role, or whether he even liked it.

Anyway, while McKeown was managing the inner crime scene, he was one of the best at it. Nothing got past him, not even the fact Lauren's crime scene goggles weren't attached properly. 'Sarge, you'll need to tighten those.'

'Of course.'

Cullen was used to wearing masks now, but the way everything clung to his sweaty skin still didn't feel right. 'Ready?'

Lauren adjusted her goggles again. 'Ready.'

'Thanks, Malky.' Cullen nodded at McKeown, then stepped under the crime scene tape. Not even a breeze to make it flap. His phone thrummed in his pocket. A text from Hunter. *No sign of Geddes at her home.*

Cullen sighed as he tapped out his reply: *Tell your sergeant, Craig, not me.* He pocketed his phone and looked around and didn't know the collective noun for CSIs. Murder seemed appropriate, but that was crows. Whatever it was, they were grouped together, searching, dusting whatever they found, then cataloguing and bagging, all up in the middle of a small cave. A few metres across of bare rock blasted away to an opening. And there was a bugger of a climb to get up there.

'Come on.' Cullen set off, but the bootees covering his shoes didn't exactly give much traction.

Lauren was way ahead of him, taking long strides and staying stable, so stable that she held out a hand to haul Cullen up. Deceptively strong too.

He got onto a flatter section, just along from the cave opening, and checked the five bodies jammed into the space.

Cullen could recognise Jimmy Deeley's belly a mile off, even through fog and at night. The Edinburgh pathologist was crouched down, working away. But whatever he saw, he was shaking his head at it. And most importantly of all, blocking what he was looking at.

'Coming through.' Cullen stepped through the CSIs huddled this side of Deeley, then had to stop dead.

Just under the overhang, a body lay on a pedestal of rough, natural stone, and naked. Definitely a woman, but her face was a red mess that didn't look human. Cullen caught glimpses of blonde hair in amongst the horror. He had to step away.

Not that the mask offered him much fresh air.

'You okay, Scott?' Lauren was next to him, head tilted to the side.

'I'll be fine.'

Someone had done that to another human being. That level of ferocity and rage. Jesus Christ. He needed to catch them. It was the only way to block it out.

'I'll be good, Lauren. Can you go and find who discovered the body?'

'Think it was a dog walker. Speaking to uniform.'

'All the same. Wouldn't be the first time, would it?'

'No.' Her cheeks dimpled through the goggles and she passed him with a pat on the arm.

Just that gentle touch brought Cullen back.

The cave wasn't quite off the beaten track, and the lockdown exercise allowance of an hour and locally meant that it probably limited the number of people hiking nearby, so maybe the body had been there a while. The wounds to her face still looked fresh, though.

'Ah, young Skywalker.' Deeley joined him at the cave's entrance. 'Bit of a Batcave vibe here, isn't it? Not that there's much room for a Batmobile or a supercomputer. Makes you yearn for old Brian Bain and his constant Batman references.' He frowned. 'Actually, he stopped them a while ago, didn't he?'

'Think so.' Cullen couldn't bring himself to banter about Bain. 'You getting anything?'

'Well, she's dead.'

That hit Cullen in the gut. A joke shaped like a bullet. He couldn't stop the laugh. 'It's definitely a she?'

'Appears to be, aye.' Deeley winced. 'But good luck identifying her. All I can offer you is she's a female, early forties, hair dyed by the looks of it.' His eyes narrowed through the goggle. 'And I'd believe it's a salon dye job giving way to a home packet to touch up the roots.'

'You an expert?'

'Having to become one, aye. Number of deaths we've had during lockdown that've been like that. Of course, there are a few that have clearly been to an illicit salon.'

'That's it?'

'No, I've got her National Insurance number tattooed on the inside of her thigh.'

One of the CSIs waved at Deeley. 'There is a tattoo.'

'What?' Deeley raised his hands. 'Why didn't you say?'

'Like you'd listen, you old goat.' Or at least it sounded like that. The CSI — who Cullen thought might or might not have been James Anderson, though there was no trace of his telltale goatee — pointed at the shoulder. Through a splatter of blood, was a fresh-looking tattoo in Chinese symbols.

Deeley was shaking his head at it. 'What's that mean?'

'Ran it through a translator app on my phone. Amazing what you can get now, eh? It means "Good Girl".'

'Huh.' Even through his mask, Deeley was wide-eyed. Whether at the victim's tattoo or the phone's technology, Cullen didn't know.

So he nudged him. 'Cause of death?'

'Murder.'

'Very funny, but I'm really not in the mood.'

'Well, Skywalker, unless there's a werewolf around here or a pack of wild wolves, I'd say a human being did that to her face with a machete.'

'You're sure about that?'

'I know machetes, Scott. Been on a few walking holidays to parts of Africa and South America where you need one to get through the vegetation and to fight off the local predators.'

'Hear they're wanting to reintroduce wolves to Scotland.' Elvis was getting suited up down below. The nosy sod could pick up a muffled chat through masks at five hundred yards.

'Heard that too, aye.' Deeley gave the wide-eyed nod of a man not wanting to seem to patronise his listener as he patronised his listener. 'But, Paul, that's purported to be in the Highlands, not down here in Midlothian. Not even talking about doing it in the Borders. And they don't have approval to do any of it.'

Elvis put his goggles on, but left them stuck to his forehead like he was going flying in the forties. 'But it looked like a wolf, did it?'

'No, Paul, it was a machete, like I told Scott here.'

'Right. What about any identifying marks?'

'Can't find any. Other than her tattoo. Not even ear piercings. I'll submit the DNA right away, but we've got staff shortages like you wouldn't believe. It'll be a long delay, I'm afraid.'

Cullen had that feeling deep in his gut, where things on a

case joined with other things. Must be some brain-gut flora connection going on.

'Come on, Jimmy, I need an ID here.'

'Sorry, Scott, but I have literally no latitude. The government want data all the time from us, and I'm talking UK government and Scottish too. There's no way I can prioritise a murder over widespread public safety.'

So Cullen had to rely on old-fashioned police work rather than technical wizardry. He got out his phone.

Shepherd calling...

'Scott, it's Luke. Sorry, I missed you earlier, just wanted to arrange a quick catch-up.'

'Okay, I'm a bit tied up just now. I'm at a murder scene in Midlothian.' Cullen glanced at the corpse inside the cliff. 'Have you found Geddes?'

'No.' Shepherd sighed down the line. 'Got a meeting with an idiot, so I'll catch you later. Cheers, Scott.' And he was gone.

What a waste of time. But Shepherd was the kind of guy who liked to keep an eye on people, wasn't he?

Cullen pocketed his phone and looked around. Everything seemed bleached to black and white by the bright sun. He flicked his hand towards Elvis. 'Have you got the CCTV yet?'

'Well, aye, I've spoken to the boy but—'

'Why are you still here, Paul?'

'Well, the boy in Dalkeith won't let me see any of it without your approval.'

'So you decided to trample over a crime scene?' Cullen held his gaze. 'Get over there, then get them to phone me or Lauren.'

'Fine.' Elvis started undoing his suit. He threw the goggles into the discard pile and stormed off in a huff.

'Can't get the staff, eh?' Deeley smirked through his own goggles. 'And the thing I haven't told you, Scott? That's a doozer.'

Cullen held Deeley's gaze. 'What?'

Deeley ran a hand over his face mask and googles. 'Those wounds didn't kill her.'

'What did?'

'Remember a few years back, we had a case where I had to

demonstrate a strangulation technique on DI Bain, as was. Well, it's similar. But...'

'But what?'

'Well, there's a lot of marks around her neck. Like she's been strangled a lot.'

'Like, this took a lot of killing?'

'No, the bruising goes back a few weeks.'

'So, a sex thing?'

'That, or she's been held captive. I mean, I know you always want to head to the pervert aisle...' Deeley clicked both fingers. 'But that's a working assumption for us to confirm. I'll be a few more minutes, then I'll give you a time of death, okay?'

'Didn't even have to ask. Thanks, Jimmy.' Cullen watched him shuffle back into the cave and got a horrible shiver down his spine.

Dying in a place like this was bad enough, but the state of her. That was a painful death.

But it was like a pedestal. Couldn't see it from below, but from up here, it was like an offering to the gods.

He had to look away from the cave.

Only to see a face he hadn't seen for a few years. Stuart Murray was talking to Lauren by McKeown's perimeter. Bit fitter-looking than the last time, but he'd grown a ludicrous beard, as big as any cop was allowed, and wiry ginger hair poked around the sides of his mask.

Cullen set off towards them, tugging at his mask and goggles like it could remove the image of the victim seared into his brain. 'Is that Santa Claus?'

'Christ, I'm not that grey, am I?' Murray smoothed down his beard, but he was smiling at Cullen. 'How you doing, Scott?'

'Good. Ish. How's Midlothian treating you?'

'Well, the good thing is I'm a DS for Lothians & Scottish Borders division.' Murray stepped away from Lauren towards the crime tape. 'The bad thing is I'm a DS for Lothians & Scottish Borders division.'

Cullen laughed. 'Why did they choose that name? Lothian and Borders was fine, but this just confuses things.'

'All one force now, eh?'

'True. You First Attending?'

'One of my lads was, as it happens. Weird thing about us having to go into uniform through lockdown. Means we end up giving you mugs in the Edinburgh MIT our sloppy seconds.'

Cullen knew Murray's tell, that way he was tugging at his ear. 'So what were you doing out here, really?'

'Just the usual, Scott. Nothing fancy.'

Lauren joined them, her hair now hanging free. 'Stuart introduced me to the dog walker who found the body.'

'Anything?'

'One Neil Harrison of Gorebridge. Mid-forties. Walking out first thing this morning. His oldest collie ran off, and he found her in the cave, looking at the body.'

'Just looking?'

'Aye, says she's a good girl. And I believe him. Collies are smart dogs.'

'When was this?'

'Half six, he reckons. Lauren's got Eva Law sitting with him, getting the data off his smartwatch.'

Deeley chucked his medicine bag at Cullen's feet, close enough to endanger his toes even through these boots. 'Well, by my calculations, our victim—whoever she is—was murdered on Friday night.'

'Ah shite.' Murray shut his eyes. 'That's all I need.'

Cullen got between them. 'What is?'

'Look, the reason we were here, the reason this Neil Harrison lad found us and we were able to secure the place is...' Murray smoothed down his curly beard again. 'It's actually really bloody complicated. The park has been locked down throughout, and it's only just reopened today as a trial run as things go back to something like normal. Trouble is, one of the lads in the village took a test on Wednesday, and it came back positive yesterday. And the daft bugger won't tell the NHS where he was on Friday, so we've been brought in to do some contact tracing. Only, it turns out there was an illicit dogging event here on Friday night.'

Deeley raised his eyebrows. 'Care to tell me what dogging is?'

'You know what it is.'

Deeley had that mischievous twinkle in his eyes. 'Enlighten me.'

Murray sighed. 'People having sex in car parks, basically. Or out in the woods here.'

'So, public swinging?'

'Aye.'

'And you say Friday night?'

'I did.'

'Were you there?'

'Of course I wasn't!' Murray was blushing.

Deeley stepped under the tape and clapped his arm. 'Just messing with you, son.' He turned to face Cullen. 'Look, by my reckoning the victim was murdered in that timeframe. All these sexual deviants you're contact tracing? Well, it's possible someone saw something. Or they did it.'

Cullen shut his eyes. And the sort of person who was open about their sexuality in public among consenting adults just *loved* sharing information with the police. But something else clawed at his throat. 'And those marks around her neck?'

Deeley was nodding hard. 'Oh aye. The kind of person who likes to shag al fresco might have other kinks.'

6

This place, I swear...

     Holyrood Parliament, whatever it's officially called.
I *love* it. Heard Su— Cullen say it looks like a swimming baths in Forfar or Stranraer. And he's right, but that's kind of the point, isn't it?

Trouble with Westminster is it's in London, and full of all that Houses of Parliament and Big Ben nonsense, all that ancient pomp and ceremony. How's someone in Wigan or Lincoln or South Shields, or even Forfar or Stranraer, how are they supposed to relate to all of that? Eh?

This place, though, it does what it says on the tin. Even though the boy who designed it was from Barca, it looks like Scotland, serves Scotland.

Bosh!

Still, that chump Hunter has persuaded the security boy to open up, so it's 'mask on' time. Standard-issue pale blue, rather than the Spider-Man one that makes my wee lassie coo and giggle when I wear it. Fatherhood has changed us, I tell you. Well, second time's a charm. First was a complete disaster.

Hunter holds the door for us. 'Ever dance with the devil in the pale moonlight?'

I've got quite good at telling when someone's speaking even with a mask on, but what did he say? 'You what?'

'What was difficult about that?'

'You said, "Ever dance with the devil in the pale moonlight?" The Joker's line from that Michael Keaton *Batman* film.'

'No, I said, "Haven't heard you call Scott Sundance in months." And I still haven't.'

'I'm a changed man, Craig. Stopped swearing too.'

'Holy shit.' His eyes go wide, like he's just realised. 'Why?'

'The little lady persuaded us. Said it was undermining me.'

Seriously, though, this place makes me wish I was allowed to swear. It's beautiful. No matter how municipal the parly looks on the outside, it's staggering inside. Surely Cullen would even agree with me. Like the poshest hotels, or those headquarter buildings for RBS or Alba Bank. And I've been in both. It's that level of care and attention to detail that's going on here.

Call it a concourse, don't they? Place could fit thousands in here. Probably enough for all the MSPs and the staff and a couple of schools' worth of visiting kids to fill up, and to get out in an emergency.

And it's not that echo-y either, could hear a pin drop.

Magnificent. Puts a real lump in your throat.

And there's old Budgie, waiting for us by the staircase up. English, eh? Suppose I can call him that rather than Buxton, as it's Cullen's nickname for him, not mine. That's not against the rules.

Shepherd's talking to him. Well, whispering more like. Can't pick up what he's saying.

Leaving Buxton fiddling with his falsers. Pair of teeth at the front, from when the daft sod tumbled through a door that someone opened.

I follow Hunter over. 'You okay, Simon?'

'These are really bloody sore today.' Buxton starts off up the stairs, his shoes clicking like that smiling boy in all those dancing films.

'You not getting implants?'

'Dentists are only doing emergency work just now. Got to wait until August, they reckon. At least.'

'Can't you go private?'

'It's the politics of the thing.' Buxton stops at the top and pulls up his mask to fiddle with his falsers. It's like looking into an alien thing on a sci-fi film. Makes me sick.

'What was Shepherd after?'

'Like I'm going to tell you.' Buxton grins at us, all sinister with those gnashers, then he flips his mask back down.

I clap him on the arm. 'Still, I bet you wish your bird had missing teeth like that, eh? Shove that—'

'Stop!' Hunter grabs my shoulder and it's like that wee alien bugger has clamped on. Sore as hell. 'Enough!'

'I'm just having a la—AAAAGH!'

Boy twists his nails in. 'Think about it. Nobody wants their ... bits talked about, okay? Big, small, bent, straight or lumpy. So stop it.'

No way am I giving him the satisfaction.

'And he's a person, okay? Stop reducing him to his parts.'

'You're always pissing in the cubicles, Craig. Can you—'

'Shut up!'

Ow, my whole arm's on fire, not just my wrist. 'Aye, aye, I'll quit it.'

And he lets go.

But Shepherd's clocked us. Boy always looks suspicious, but this time he's onto us. Onto Hunter's bullying anyway.

He's with some lad who's seven foot tall, if a day. And he looks young, a dusting of dark stubble to make him appear a bit older than twelve.

I shake Hunter's grip off. 'Come on, boys, let's at least look professional.' Have to adjust my mask as that chump has knocked it. Don't want some jobsworth in here fining us or, worse, reporting us for it.

'Gentlemen.' Shepherd's nostrils are flared wide as we approach. Thank God this isn't going to be a long-term thing, as Shepherd has clearly already got the measure of what a bunch of choppers he's dealing with. 'This is Ms Geddes's PA. Deacon Abercrombie. He called in the disappearance.'

Deacon...

When did surnames become first names? 'Hi guys.' His voice has that depth, like it's just broken. 'So, as I was saying to your boss here, Isobel is usually in before six. Isobel's a workaholic, so my job is about removing distractions from work. I get here just after, make sure she's got everything she needs, then I just let her get on with it and field calls and yadda yadda yadda.'

Boy might have the looks of someone singing soprano in the choir, but he seems to know his onions. And garlic and shallots and red onions and leeks, too.

And none of the other chumps here are jumping in, so I suppose I'd better. 'But she isn't in work today?'

'Right. I called it in.' Deacon's scratching at his face mask. Something's got him rattled. 'I was worried, you know? She cycles in, and I thought maybe she'd been hit on the way? But no, there weren't any reports of that, so they put me on to you guys. And... Well.'

Feel a bit weird standing out here in the corridor, but it's not like there's anybody actually about, is there?

'I mean, I thought what if someone's kidnapped her?' Deacon's looking at Shepherd.

Who just nods. 'We'll consider that as a distinct possibility. But without any demands received, it's hard to assess if that's viable.'

'You think she could have just disappeared?'

Shepherd nods. Cool as a cucumber, this boy.

'Why?'

'She's got a stressful job, Deacon. It stands to reason, doesn't it? The world is falling apart. All of the pressure placed on a minister. And it must be constant just now. Sure, the school year will officially end in a month or so, but she's got to make sure homeschooling is working, and all the while there's economic pressure to get kids back so parents can be more productive, and there's the health aspects. That's enough to drive anyone to the edge.'

'Not Isobel.'

'How so?'

'Stress is what she thrives on.' Deacon doesn't look so sure now. There's making someone's coffees and doing their filing, then there's knowing them. And I think he probably makes noises about how well he knows her, but at the end of the day, while the kid might go on to great things, right now he is just making her coffee and doing her filing. He doesn't know what makes Isobel Geddes's mind tick.

But he's distracted by a man walking past us, splitting this daft group down the middle, and sauntering into an office like he owns the place.

Shepherd follows the boy's path. 'Who's that, Deacon?'

'The party's lead lawyer, basically.'

'Okay.' Shepherd folds his arms. 'Did Isobel ever mention Gorebridge to you?'

What the hell? Has he finally cracked?

Deacon shakes his head. 'Not to me.'

'Gore Glen?'

'Uh no.'

'What about Midlothian?'

'Well, isn't Edinburgh in Midlothian?'

'Not for a long time. Edinburgh's Edinburgh. South of the bypass, pretty much, it's Midlothian until the Borders.'

'Well, she never really mentioned it. There was a school visit at Penicuik in November.'

'Nothing since?'

'Afraid not.'

'Okay.' Shepherd smiles at Deacon, then pats Buxton on the arm. 'Can you work with Simon and Craig here, dig out any colleagues or friends or family that you know of, anyone who could've heard from Ms Geddes over the weekend, that kind of thing?'

'I've been on to them all morning. Nobody's heard from or seen her since Friday.'

'Even so.' Shepherd does that trick I used to do, holds the boy's gaze with his eyebrows raised until the boy just has to nod and do what he's been asked to. 'Thanks.' And he nods at me. 'Lead on, Big Muff.'

'Big Muff?'

'I said McDuff. It's from Shakespeare.'

'Right.' But it sounded a lot like he called me Big Muff. And I know how nicknames stick, so if that one lingers, he's getting it in the neck. With a letter opener. Anyway, I man up and lead the big bugger into the office.

Place is absolute chaos. Papers everywhere. Two laptops and a desktop PC. Bookshelves rammed with papers and documents and not many books, have to say. Cracking view across to Holyrood House, mind, not that Her Majesty is in residence just now.

Christ knows where she is, actually. Probably Windsor? Maybe up at Glamis, riding this whole thing out. Smart move of her. Got a lot of time for the Queen, have to say.

And the baldie boy is rummaging around on her desk, going through the papers like he's after something.

'Can I help you, sir?'

He takes one look at us, and frowns. Daft sod isn't wearing a mask. Can't think if 'lanky' covers how tall the boy is, but he's even bigger than Deacon outside there, and he's got a similar boyishness about him. Maybe they're related. Actually a good thing he's got his mask off as I can see the port wine stain on his cheek, like a drop of sperm with a long bloody tail. Makes him extremely distinctive, though.

And the cheeky sod goes back to his search like there aren't two cops in his office. 'I'll be done soon.'

'You're done now, sir. DC Brian Bain. This is—'

'This is important.' He's sitting now, tossing documents all over the place. And shaking his head with a face like his poodle has rolled shite all over the carpet in the holiday home he's staying in.

'Sir, this is a police matter.' Despite his size, Shepherd's over there in a flash, getting between the lad and his precious paperwork. 'For starters, I need you to put that mask around your mouth and nose.'

That gets him. He looks up at us with a snidey sneer. 'You're wearing masks. You'll be fine.'

'It's not about us, sir.' Shepherd pings the strap on his own mask. 'These are to stop us transmitting it to you. You can still transmit it to us.'

'This is a bunch of malarkey.' The chump slumps back in the chair. 'Complete malarkey.'

'Be that as it may, sir, I still need to know what you're up to here. Let's start with your name, shall we?'

Boy's searching the desk with his eyes, not paying attention to Shepherd. 'Peter Tomlinson, head of Legal Affairs for our party. Where the hell is it?'

Unlike Shepherd, I keep my two-metre distance. 'What are you looking for, sir?'

He gives up his hunt and actually tucks his mask on. 'Isobel is an obsessive printer. Everything gets printed out. Emails, documents, you name it, whatever it is, if she's received it, it's getting printed.'

'Even text messages on her—?'

'She doesn't text.'

'Doesn't text? Eh?'

'Just doesn't do it. It's all email. All about the audit trail.' Tomlinson huffs out a sigh. 'So I've been trying to unpick any bookings she might've made.'

'To find out where she's gone this weekend?'

'Indeed. But there's nothing.' Tomlinson pushes up to standing and goes over to the window. More shaking of his head. His lockdown haircut isn't the best. Boy must be glad he's not in court soon. 'It's only eight thirty, but I've already spent hours today speaking to people at the *Argus*.'

'The paper? Why?'

Tomlinson sighs. 'Because we have sources there.' He looks up at the ceiling, like there are spiders up there or something. Sour look on his face, either way. 'They told us the paper was going to run a story.'

'A story?'

'Aye. I spoke to them and had it shifted from the Sunday edition.' He scratches at his mask again. 'Only for it to turn up in this morning's *Argus*.' He nods over to the desk.

I'm nearest, and it doesn't take us long to find it. That morning's *Argus*, barely read, barely even creased.

"DOUBLE STANDARDS"

One of those telephoto shots of a woman getting out of a car and looking all shifty as she reties a long scarf. They must take hundreds of them and spend ages poring through looking for the absolute worst one. Got to love the press, eh?

I scan the text, and it looks like an exposé on Isobel Geddes using her second home in the Borders during lockdown. Every Friday night until Monday morning, when some of the other photos show her at her pad in Porty.

Well, that gives the other side of old Maureen's journal. Maybe there's a Maureen down in the Borders keeping another log.

I hand the paper over to Shepherd, but keep my peace.

Tomlinson is still fiddling with his mask. 'A lot of countries haven't locked down as hard as we have, like Sweden, say, and some were a lot worse, like China and Italy. Either way, it's not a good look for the Schools Minister to be ignoring the rules, especially when there's bound to be an absolute farrago come August and exam result season.'

Shepherd plonks the paper back on the desk. 'So was that your goal?'

'What?'

'Well, keep the story hidden until August, then you'll have an easy patsy for the inevitable disaster.'

'That's a baseless accusation.'

'No, it's not.' Shepherd looks right at him and Tomlinson wilts under the heat. 'Because you're not telling us the complete truth, are you?'

'You know, don't you?'

And of course, neither Shepherd nor Tomlinson are telling me what they're talking about. I'd point that out, but I doubt they'd stop it.

Shepherd nods. 'Deacon told me.'

'Little sod.' Tomlinson leans back against the glass. 'Then, I'll be honest with you. There's a slight conflict of interest here. I'm Isobel's ex-husband.'

Bingo. Suspect number one. Ex-husband looking for something. Maybe too obvious, but then again, I've been caught out like that before.

'So you know her well. She have friends in Gorebridge?'

Tomlinson snarls like Shepherd's pissed all over his shoes. '*Gorebridge?*'

'No need to say it like that, sir.'

'Heavens, no. It's not part of her greater ward, either.'

'When was the last time you saw Isobel?'

'Months ago. She's devoted to her position here, and can be frosty.'

'Frosty?'

'She pushes people away. You don't rise up in the party without having laser-like focus on your career. Embarrassments such as myself can be easily forgotten and paved over.'

'Paved over? That's a curious expression.'

'Sorry, it's just a turn of phrase. Everyone in Isobel's life is a stepping stone, but she makes sure what's behind her is paved over.'

'You seem to have some malice towards her.'

'I really don't. Our divorce was just mutual apathy. We wanted to see other people. End of story.'

'And is she?'

'What?'

'Seeing other people.'

'Not that I'm aware of.' Tomlinson picked up the paper. 'The journalist seems to know somewhat more of her life than I ever did.'

7

M urray was waiting, standing by his car, arms folded,
eyebrows raised. 'Pampas grass.' He was pointing to
the side.

Cullen shut his door and checked the address.

A post-war semi, harled in beige-brown, but with a cracking
view across to the new housing development spreading this
way. A dog-walking path ran to the side, but the parking area
was filled with Cullen's car and a squad car, with its Battenberg
Police Scotland livery. The drive had a work van and a souped-
up blue Clio, the kind that wee dickheads would hurtle around
B-roads in.

And sure enough, slap bang in the middle of the lawn was a
big spidery pampas grass.

Cullen shook his head at Murray. 'That's a myth, Stuart?'

'Sure?'

'Well, I hope it is. My parents have one in the front garden.'

'Best left unsaid, eh?' Murray headed up the drive and
pulled his mask low.

The front door opened and a burly uniform stood there
with McKeown. 'Sarge.' Just that, and he was back inside.

McKeown shook his head at the closing door. 'Can't get the
staff, eh?'

'Can you get an update from Craig Hunter?'

McKeown sniffed. 'Shouldn't that be from Luke Shepherd, sir?'

'Please.' Cullen followed Murray into the house. The thing he always forgot about these houses, only to always realise when he was in one, was how they might look the same from outside, but they were all completely different inside. Some were hellholes with gardens filled with weeds and discarded shite, some were smoke dens, but this one...

One of Ryan and Dawn Marshall had an eye for decor. Everything seemed immaculate and well considered. The small hallway had little nooks and crannies cut into the walls, all filled with tasteful ornaments.

Murray followed his uniform into the living room. A pair of beige sofas sat a few feet apart, covered with purple and yellow cushions. The walls had atmospheric black-and-white photos of central Edinburgh.

Dawn sat facing two uniforms, holding her husband's hand. Her purple jumper matched the cushions perfectly, like they'd been made from the same material. She had a slight sadness in her eyes, and looked absolutely shattered. 'I mean, we're struggling with homeschooling our kids. You think three is going to be fine, don't you? But then this happens and... *You* try getting a full day's work in when you've got to make sure Daisy's doing her reading, or Sam's at his sums or Casey's—'

A racking cough burst out of Ryan. 'CHRIST!' He jerked forward and started thumping his chest. He wore a sports vest, not to show off muscles but his many tattoos, including a griffin fighting a snake on his neck. At least, that's what it looked like. And something on his left shoulder looked like it had been only partly done come lockdown. 'CHRIST!'

Dawn stroked his back, slowly. 'But if he's like this, I'll have four bairns to look after, won't I?'

Murray got one of the uniforms to clear off and took a seat on the sofa, but he kept his mask tightened. 'So it's definitely Covid-19?'

'Aye.' Ryan cleared his throat into a closed fist. He was

sweating, hard enough to soak through his pale fabric. 'Had a test. Got the results back this morning.'

Murray had his notebook splayed on his lap, like he was taking this seriously. 'Do you know where you caught it, sir?'

'I was at a boy's house, fitting a hen run for him in his garage. Inside. He was coughing and, let's just say, he wasn't social distancing.'

'You didn't try and get him to back off?'

'Course I tried.' Ryan coughed again, though it wasn't as hard as before. 'He wouldn't listen. Must be where I caught it.'

'And when was this?'

'Weekend before last.'

Murray nodded at his colleague. 'That fits the timeline.'

Ryan frowned at them. His arms were filled with footballer's sleeves, a mishmash of tattoos covering every inch of skin. 'What timeline?'

'Well, for infection. It's the eighteenth now, so you catching it on the eighth or ninth would fit.'

'Why are cops doing this contact tracing?'

'A good question, sir.' Murray smiled. 'Normally, we'd let Public Health Scotland take the lead, but they've had to abandon contact tracing. And we have reason to believe that you weren't the only person attending a particular event who had the virus.'

'Event? What are you talking about?'

'On Friday night.'

'We were in here on Friday. I've not passed nothing to anyone.'

'You weren't at Gore Glen?'

'Of course I wasn't!'

'Sir, it's okay to be there. We just need to know.'

'I don't have to tell you anything!'

'Mr Marshall, it'll make our jobs a lot easier if you just admit to it. And if our jobs are easier, we can stop the further spread of this bug.'

Ryan looked at his wife, but Cullen could see denial in his eyes. And in her hers. 'Fine. We were there. For a walk!' He coughed again. 'But the reason I'm a bit cagey about it is I heard some deviants were there on Friday.'

'Deviants?'

'Aye. Swingers. Weirdos. We're worried we'll get prosecuted and fined, when all we were doing was having a walk.'

'Were your kids with you?'

'They weren't, no.'

'Just the two of you?'

'What's this about?'

Cullen had already had enough. He'd seen this denial before. The shame of public sexual intercourse was what attracted people like Ryan and Dawn Marshall to it in the first place. The danger, the frisson of excitement too. 'Look, whatever you were doing there, I'm sure it was between consenting adults.' He waited until Ryan looked right at him. 'That's cool. But if you still want to deny it, then that's not fine, because people's lives are on the line here, just because of your shame.'

Ryan and Dawn looked at each other, but yep, Cullen saw more denial. A shared secret, a shared fantasy, but a shared denial.

'Okay, so you're not going to play ball. Totally understand that. But I'm looking to identify a body. A murder victim. Someone who was there likely on Friday night.' Cullen held up a finger. 'I mean, I've worked a lot of murders, but this turned even my stomach. And I want to identify her. I want to help her family understand what's happened to her. At the moment, we don't have an identity for her. Flip that around and you get a family missing someone. And I want to stop whoever did this to that poor woman from doing it again. And maybe it was just that you might've seen her on your walk, that'd help.'

And there it was, the struggle in their eyes. Wondering if they could help, but still curtailed by the shame and embarrassment.

'Was there anyone you might've seen in the park on Friday night?'

Still they didn't speak.

Time to hit the nuclear button. Cullen sat on the coffee table, blocking the uniform's view, but sitting across from Dawn

Marshall. 'You might've seen in the news how the Covid-19 infection rates are on the way down. It's good news. Maybe lockdown will be over soon and we can have some new normal. But whatever happens, until we have a vaccine for this virus, we're going to need to prevent the spread. Everyone will. Wearing masks like these will help, a bit. Social distancing too. But what's a really, really good way to spread it is having sex in public with strangers when you've got the bug.'

Ryan stomped his foot. Nailed. Then he got up and towered over Cullen. 'This is bollocks!'

Cullen was happy to sit there, let Ryan feel big and powerful, despite the crushing cough. 'What is, sir?'

'This whole thing. Making us stay in for months. Keeping our kids at home, stopping us working!'

'And yet you were fitting a hen run in someone's garage?'

Ryan slumped back in his sofa. 'It's so bloody hard. I'm self-employed and it's an absolute pittance what they've given us. A *pittance.* I had to get out and earn. I've got kids to pay for and things are always so tight and, CHRIST, it's all well and good the politicians saying we should stay at home, but then you see shite like the Schools Minister slipping off to her second home in bloody Stow!' He tossed a paper at Cullen. 'What's that all about?'

Cullen checked the headline. Ryan was right — it seemed like a million miles away from the Marshall's world. A huge disconnect that explained a lot of the schisms in the world. 'I don't have much in her defence, I'm sorry. It must feel terrible. You're sacrificing so much. Your income, your kids' schooling and mental health, your hobbies and interests, and someone in authority does this.'

'Aye.' Ryan was nodding. 'Exactly. And it's all a myth, it's just flu.'

Okay...

Cullen gave a flash of his eyebrows. 'Well, I've had it, sir, and I'm still not over the cough. Two months on. You've got it, and maybe you'll be okay in a few days. But you might have to go to hospital. And believe me, it's much, much worse than the flu. A lot of people have been dying from it. This is no joke.'

Ryan looked at his wife and something passed between them. Maybe Cullen had won. But that remained to be seen.

Cullen shrugged. 'Okay, so on Friday you were on your healthy walk alone in the fresh air. That certainly isn't illegal. You're allowed daily exercise, after all. Going to the glen? Well, it was shut but they were opening it on Monday, right? And you're not outwith the hour of exercise. And then if you suddenly became amorous, why, that's just nature, isn't it?'

Now they looked at each other and Cullen saw a hunger in their eyes. Yep, that was the least of what they were up to. 'It was something like that.'

'I mean, maybe you saw her on this excursion. Whatever was going on.'

Dawn sat forward, hands clasped together. 'The kids have been a nightmare since lockdown. It's been bedlam. And then they let us have my parents into the garden. So we thought they could look after them for a bit... Well. And one thing led to another when we were out.'

Murray lurched to his feet. 'When you were doing this, did you notice anyone else who was out for a similar healthy? Did they notice you?'

'Stop judging us. It's nature.'

'But you were dogging, weren't you?'

Dawn shot daggers at Murray. 'That's so crass.'

'It is crass. Swinging, dogging, whatever. You were doing it.'

Cullen held up a hand to shut up Murray. 'There would be no prosecution of something so minor. The problem is, you have probably spread coronavirus to over twenty people. You might not go out much, fair enough, but if someone goes to visit their elderly father this afternoon when we could've prevented it? Well, that's on your conscience. Those deaths are on you. Because it won't just be one. It'll be many.'

Ryan looked at Cullen now. 'This woman, how can we help? You got a photo?'

'If I did, I couldn't even show you.'

Ryan ran a hand down his face.

Cullen sat forward on his seat. 'All we have is it was a woman in her early forties. Dyed her hair blonde.'

Dawn frowned. 'Look, let's just say there was a woman who wore a mask to a few of these ... events we went to. It might be her.'

'You know her name?'

'No.' Dawn grabbed her husband's hand. 'Ryan knows who organises these events. Maybe that guy recognises her.'

8

Quite a smashing view from up here, have to say.

Calton Hill towers above us, catching the light, towering over the parliament. Almost beautiful.

We're up on the *Argus*'s roof garden, and it's actually a lovely day but windy as fu— all hell.

Christ, am I allowed to say "hell" these days?

And this fanny doesn't know how good he's got it. Alan Lyall. Sure there's a joke in there somewhere, but I've turned over a new leaf, haven't I?

Scrawny wee git, like, and with a real evil look in his eyes. Swear I could argue with you all day long about whether evil's innate or not—and you *know* which side I'd be on—but this boy would be the first piece I'd put into evidence. Just get him up on the stands and one look at his coupon is enough to persuade any reluctant jurors.

He's sitting there acting all casual, when most people would be terrified of two cops showing up. Then again, this boy looks experienced and he is a journalist. Been around the blocks a few times with clowns like Shepherd, knows how to play them.

Well, wait till he gets a load of me!

'We probably shouldn't be working in an office, no, but some of us are deemed essential.'

Shepherd shifts his metal chair again, the foot grinding off the concrete slabs. I mean, they're not exactly comfy, but Christ, it's like he's inside an Iron Maiden or something. 'Looks like it's just you, though.'

'Couple of us.' Lyall twangs his face mask. 'Got to wear this all day, wash our hands every half an hour, sanitise every fifteen minutes. Absolute ball-ache. And meeting you out here at much greater than the social distancing guidelines.'

I'm about ten metres away from the boy, not two. Still feels too far. Afraid I might catch evil from him. 'Okay, but we just need to find Ms Geddes.'

'*Dr* Geddes.' Lyall grins at Shepherd. 'Nope. But she's a right arse about making sure people use that title.'

'She been an arse with you?'

'Had to cover school stories as part of my beat. Sat down with her a few times. So aye, she's been an arse with me.'

'We're just looking for some help finding her.'

'No, you're looking for my sources on this story, and you're looking to access my reporting.'

'She's a missing person.'

'So?' Lyall runs his tongue across his lips. 'You know why sources are confidential, right? It's to protect them, and to make sure the truth comes out.'

Shepherd's nodding along with it. 'Wouldn't want it any other way.'

'So you'll appreciate me not divulging any names.'

Shepherd is still nodding. Does he think that's endearing? Who knows. 'What is there to protect, though?'

'Where do I know you from?' Lyall's looking right at me. These days, I'm trying to keep a low profile, but this boy is more interested in me than Cullen would be in a single mother. 'Sure our paths have crossed somewhere.'

I give the boy a shrug. Play this right and I can show this fanny Shepherd a thing or three. Might be useful to have allies in the wider MIT, anyway. 'I've got one of those faces.'

'Nah, it's not that.' Lyall clicks his fingers a few times. 'You weren't working in Dundee a few months ago, were you?'

'That?' I give the boy a shake of the head, not too much, just enough to show some irritation, enough to show I'm on his side of the coin. 'Less said about that the better.'

Lyall flicks his eyebrows up. 'Tell me about it.'

I slide the morning's paper over the table. The newsroom in this place used to be busier than Ibrox at ten to three on a Saturday, but out here, even with that bloody wind, it's not that you can hear a pin drop so much as a sexy police officer sliding a newspaper across a desk at a distance of ten metres. I tap the front page. 'We're interested in this piece you did on Isobel Geddes.' Calling it a piece rather than a hatchet job is bound to buy some brownie points. 'Turns out Dr Geddes is now missing.'

'You don't say.' Lyall lets out a sigh. 'Look, are you suggesting my piece has driven her away?'

'Not in the literal sense, no. But in the figurative? Maybe.'

'You don't think this is an important story to get out there?'

'Not our place to judge, sir. We're merely responding to a missing persons report. Now, normally, that'd be the responsibility of our uniformed colleagues, but when it's the Schools Minister and the whole nation is under lockdown? Different kettle of fish, eh?' I give the boy a wee bit of a breather. Two big cops hitting him hard must feel like a bit of an imposition. 'Just need to know if you've had any contact with her recently.'

'Wednesday.'

'Here?'

'Outside Holyrood.' Lyall looks over at the parliament. Probably not too far away from her office, as it happens. Strange how things end up like that, isn't it? 'It was like that unstoppable force meets immovable object thing. She wouldn't talk on the phone, or even on neutral territory. So I had to bite the bullet to visit her, risking life and limb. Place is absolutely rife with Covid, I swear.'

'Take it you asked her about this piece?'

'Refused to comment on the story, didn't she?'

'So she knew about it?'

Lyall sniffed. 'Sometimes in this job, you realise when you've been played. A story like this, I was hoping to get her on the record, maybe force an apology or resignation.'

'But?'

'But she doubled down. Pushed back against it. Not so much as denied it, but... The trouble with Holyrood is it gives them an unwarranted sense of entitlement. Bottom line, Dr Isobel Geddes played politics with it.'

'How so?'

'I messed up. Told her too much. So, their party leader called my boss, got her to spike the story.' Lyall raises his forefinger exactly on the last syllable. 'Before you ask, I don't know how. Way above my pay grade, isn't it? Horse-trading they call it. Probably see a flurry of interesting stories break over the next few days and weeks.'

I'm nodding along here, but there's so much unsaid by this boy. 'Problem is, the fact that your bosses here have published this morning shows you didn't get the quid pro quo you were after.'

'Again, that's way above my pay grade.'

I make eye contact with Shepherd. Credit to the lad, he's letting me get on with this, rather than taking over like some other cops might. 'Well, Luke, turns out we're talking to the wrong boy. This lad doesn't know much about his own story.'

Oldest trick in the book and it still works like a treat.

Lyall shakes his head, looks a bit pissed off with us. 'It's not that. My understanding is the story was supposed to go out yesterday. Big Sunday splash, get her on the morning interview shows. Way I hear it, though, the party's chief lawyer got wind of the impending publication and put in a call.' And that checks out with Tomlinson's story. 'Don't know how, it wasn't me who leaked, but I was told it was put in a holding pattern. Then it came out.'

'Sounds like when your bosses didn't get anything back, they ran it?'

'That's a fair assumption to make.'

'This lawyer boy, you deal with him?'

'He called me on Saturday. I told him I couldn't do anything about the story.'

'Passed it up the ranks?'

'Right.'

'You know he's Dr Geddes's ex-husband, right?'

'Right.' Can see the boy's fingers twitching, desperate to type on his keyboard. File that one before lunchtime and make poor Tomlinson look like a right dickhead.

Shepherd leans forward and rubs his hands together. 'We're not really interested in political intrigue, though. We just want to find Dr Geddes.' He grabs the paper and runs his finger around a photo of her on Friday night, still with that scarf wrapped around her neck. 'You know who took this?'

'It wasn't me.'

'Not what I asked.'

Lyall does a little weird little thing with his eyes, where they kind of roll. If it went on any longer, I'd think he was having a stroke or something. He waves his paw over at the steps we had to climb to get up here. Rickety would be generous.

But they've barely rattled, and this other skinny bugger is walking over the rooftop, with a pair of fancy headphones around his neck catching the light. Takes us a few seconds, but I think I know him. Richard McAlpine.

Cullen used to live with him, but not like that. Flatmates. As far as I know, anyway.

He stands between me and Lyall. 'What's this about?'

'Cops here are asking about the Geddes story.'

'Right.' Rich does not look like a happy bunny, at all. Standing so far away that it's really bloody hard to make him out over the wind. Boy's a whisperer, that's for sure. 'What about it?'

Lyall sits back down, seeming a bit more at ease now that he's shared the blame around. 'Rich did a lot of the work on this too, especially on her background. His photo, too.'

Rich just stands there, supermodel thin. Bones for arms where there should be muscle. Least he's grown his hair out a bit. 'Alan, I'm taking the rap for this.'

'There's no rap to take, Rich. Come off it.' Lyall sits back and twangs his mask again. 'Look, we got a tip-off from a concerned citizen in Stow.' Bingo, old Maureen's southern cousin. 'Neighbour of Dr Geddes reported strange weekend comings and goings. So the pair of us took turns watching Dr Geddes's home in Stow over the weekends. See her arriving on a Friday, leaving early on a Monday.'

Rich stares at us, clearly knows who I am, but doesn't say anything. 'I was there on Friday night.'

'And you saw her?'

'Well, yeah. The photo's in the paper, you chump.'

'Chump. That's a good one.' I give him a big laugh. 'So you—'

'Aye, I saw Dr Geddes turn up. It was getting dark, so I had to use the telephoto with a flash and a slow shutter speed.'

'You took them yourselves?'

'Another cost-saving thing, isn't it? I mean, I could dig out the photos and tell you the timestamp.'

'That'd be good.' Make the old mental note to follow up. 'You see anyone?'

'Nope. Just caught her on camera and drove off.'

'Okay, and do you have any idea why she would just disappear like this?'

'I mean, yeah.' Rich sticks his tongue in his cheek. 'I mean, we're making her life a misery by running this. Wouldn't you bugger off somewhere?'

'Aye, but we're in lockdown. Where could she go?'

He just shrugs. Lyall joins in with one of his own.

'So neither of you know where she could've gone?'

'Flat in Edinburgh. Porty, I think.'

'Been there already.'

Rich shrugs. 'Then, as far as I know, she's still in that house.'

9

The A68 through Pathhead thundered with lorries and cars, like the lockdown was already over. Eight weeks of staying in except for essential trips. And that story in the morning's paper was probably another nail in the coffin, along with that Westminster adviser who drove to County Durham, the English scientist who was seeing his mistress on the sly, and the Scottish scientist travelling to Fife. Hard not to get angry with them, thinking they're above the law.

And Isobel Geddes was another one, her story filling the news. Most people would skirt the line, maybe two hour-long walks on a Sunday, or going to the shops twice, but when you're in the spotlight, it's the worst thing you can do.

Cullen drove on, but lockdown meant the village was a ghost town. But things had picked up today, with the village pub offering takeaway tea and coffee. Could probably rustle up some draught beer if you asked nicely. He pulled in between two big SUVs, one of them with two flat tyres.

Murray was sitting on the bonnet of the other one, tapping his watch.

Cullen got out and joined him. 'Had to come here a few weeks ago. Bizarre for the main road to Newcastle to be so empty.'

Murray hopped down onto the pavement. 'And you didn't call me?'

'Kind of a bit of a rush. Plus I wasn't feeling so well.'

'Oh?'

'I had Covid.'

'Shite.' Murray walked up the long path to the front door. Big old farmhouse, but the settlement had grown up around it. 'Impressive work back there. My lads have been at them and got nothing.'

Cullen peered through the replacement windows, but couldn't see past his own twisted reflection. 'It's all just "cognitive distortion" on their part.'

'What?'

'You'll know it as "Stinkin' thinkin'", or just the lies people tell themselves to justify their actions. The Marshalls wouldn't admit that they'd been dogging, but if you take each lie as it comes, you can lead them to the point where you can break the story apart in a different way. And the bottom line is I got them to admit they were there, got some potential witnesses, some definite contacts to trace. And murder trumps perversion every time.'

'Sound like you've been on a course.'

'Just you wait until you're a DI, Stuart. It never ends. Day job takes up all your time, then they expect you to attend courses in the evenings.'

'Well, that'll be a long—'

The door opened to a crack and an eye peered out, baby blue and squinting. A thin shard of cheek, covered in stubble. 'What?'

'Wayne Leonard?'

'Aye?'

'Police, sir.' Murray held out his warrant card. 'Need to ask you a few questions.'

'Just a sec.' Leonard disappeared and the door opened from an inch to a foot. Leonard had a thick beard and hair piled up on top. Mid-forties, maybe. 'Sorry, you can't come in. I'm not well.' And there it was, an eruption of the Covid cough. Leonard had to double over to get it out of his system.

If Cullen hadn't been through it himself, he would've suspected some tearing to the lungs. 'Coronavirus?'

'Tested positive yesterday.' Another wracking cough.

'Sorry to hear that, sir.' Murray adjusted his face mask. 'Do you know where you caught it?'

'Complete mystery, pal.'

'When did the symptoms first appear?'

'Woke up on Saturday and felt a bit crappy. Got worse from there. Sunday, I was coughing my guts up.'

'You woke up here on Saturday?'

Leonard frowned at Murray. 'What's that supposed to mean?'

'It means, you might've caught the virus on Friday night.'

'No, I think the incubation period is a bit longer than that.'

'Okay, so say it was from the previous Saturday, any idea—'

'Why are two cops pitching up on my doorstep?'

'We're doing contact tracing, sir.'

'Contact tracing?'

'It's become part of the job just now. Helping out where we can, especially when there's an outbreak that requires absolute truth.'

'Right.'

'So where were you on Friday night?'

'Well, I was here.'

'Alone?'

Leonard sighed. 'You trying to suggest I wasn't?'

'You a married man?'

'Not any more.'

'Sir, we're contact tracing from a meeting in Gore Glen on Friday night. If you were there, you might've been passing on the coronavirus asymptomatically. We need to confirm your whereabouts in the evening. Say you went for a walk with a friend. Socially distanced.'

'Bugger off.' Leonard slammed the door.

Cullen winced at Murray. 'Looks like you need to book yourself on that course, Stuart.'

'Aye, aye.' Murray ran a hand down his face, briefly

displacing his mask. 'Right, if he's started getting symptoms, then the stupid sod has probably passed it on to the other perverts. I need to update our contact tracing log.'

'Assuming he was there.'

'Oh, I think that's safe to assume.' Murray shook his head. 'Why do people have to be so bloody weird?'

Cullen smiled. 'Nothing wrong about having sexual peccadillos, Stuart. Sure you've got a few of your own.'

'No I don't.'

'Aye? So you'll let me see your internet search history?'

That got him, judging by the redness climbing his neck.

Cullen held out a hand. 'Go. I'll see if I can get him to open up.'

'Cheers, mate.' Murray walked off, phone to his head.

Leaving Cullen standing outside the home of the ringleader of a dogging group who had passed the bug on. Superspreading that didn't bear thinking about.

He knocked on the door and checked for movement inside.

In normal circumstances, it would be slightly funny, maybe.

But these selfish arseholes were causing people to die. Not that they couldn't keep it in their pants. Then again, for a lot of them dogging was a spectator sport, a sex show in public. But being in public was the problem, the last thing they should be doing.

Cullen needed to stop thinking like that. He had a goal here. Identify a dead body. And he had a lead who might help with that. Focus, use his training and nail this idiot. He rapped on the door again.

It clattered open. Leonard was wearing green hiking trousers with padding in all the right places, and a few of the wrong ones, like his crotch. His plain white T-shirt was stained with egg yolk and possibly coffee. 'What now?'

'Sir, we really need your help here.'

'I told you to bugger off.'

'And I wish I could. The last thing I want to be doing is hassling someone about dogging.'

'*Dogging*?'

'Sexual inter—'

'I know what it is. Do you have evidence of my involvement? No. You don't. So bugger off!'

Cullen stopped the door with his foot. 'We do have evidence, sir. Two people are on record saying you were in Gore Glen on Friday night.'

'Well, I wasn't.'

'So you were here all evening, were you?'

'I think so.'

'Sir, I know what you're going through. I have experience of suffering from Covid-19. I caught it saving someone's life two months ago. And for about a week after my test came back, I felt like I was dying. Luckily I didn't have to get hospitalised, but I came close. Do you have anyone who can look in on you?'

'Eh?'

'There are a lot of people on their own who are dying from it. It's a common thing. My girlfriend is a cop too, and she's been investigating home deaths in West Lothian.'

'Right. I've...' Leonard sighed. 'There are some friends who have been keeping in touch. People in the village.'

'That's good to hear. Do you mind if I come inside?'

Leonard frowned. 'It's an absolute guddle in there. And I've —' Another cough burst out of his lungs. He tried to catch it in his elbow, but it didn't seem to work.

'Sir, I've had it. I've had a positive antibody test and have been approved for entry into places like this.'

'Well, if you insist.' Leonard disappeared into the house.

Cullen set foot through the door and felt a shiver climb up his neck. Entering the home of a known sufferer, while he was taking only the theoretical advice of a doctor about retransmission. He couldn't go through that ordeal again. He wasn't sure he was over the first time yet.

But, as was so often the case with his career, duty overtook personal safety.

He followed Leonard inside. And he was completely right. A guddle was drastically underselling it. The place wasn't even a mess. Cullen's mother would call it a midden. The large living room was covered in rubbish. Empty pizza boxes and takeaway cartons. Discarded bottles, though nothing too boozy by the looks of it.

Yeah, Wayne Leonard needed a cleaner in here and soon. He slumped onto the sofa and looked drained of all energy. He punched at his chest on the left side, like he was trying to restart his heart.

'Can I fetch you a cup of tea or coffee, sir?'

Leonard shook his head. 'Milk went off on Friday and I haven't got anything back in.'

'A black coffee?'

'Tastes like tar, man.' Leonard coughed hard again.

Cullen felt that wave of revulsion. Must be how lion tamers felt. And they never got maimed by their animals, did they?

He picked up a roll of bin bags from the kitchen counter and pulled one out, then set about filling it with discarded rubbish. He tossed a newspaper in.

'Leave that. Haven't finished it.'

Cullen fished it out again and put it on the table. That morning's *Argus*, with the Isobel Geddes story. He looked over at Leonard. 'You've got to make sure you get enough hydration. What about some water?'

'I've had two litres today, already. Trying to flush my system.'

'Smart move.' Cullen folded two pizza boxes in half, then stuffed them inside. 'Almost filled the first bag already here.'

'Didn't ask you to.'

'So, have you been getting exercise?'

'Quite a lot actually. Been getting into fell running.'

Cullen frowned. 'Running up and down hills?'

'Right. It's big down in the Borders. Head a few miles south of here, and you're at some lovely big hills. I mean, people head down to the Tweed Valley for mountain biking, but the running is to die for.'

And Wayne Leonard seemed to be a man intent on dying young. Or in early middle age, anyway.

'You get your exercise in on Friday?'

Leonard nodded, but didn't look at Cullen.

'Sir, I get that this is hard to admit, but we know you're a member of a sex club. I'm not judging you, unless you're not doing stuff with consenting adults. Then it's a whole other thing. But if you're all grown-ups and you all agree, then who am I to judge?'

A brief flicker of eye contact, then Leonard was away, focusing on his giant TV.

'My colleague is working to contact trace people from the event. I'm sure you understand when I say that Public Health Scotland weren't making much headway. The government are looking to ease the lockdown, so it's imperative that we step in and aid their efforts. This is an incredibly serious matter, sir. If you had the coronavirus and you spread it, we need to know. Lockdown can only go so far. While Stuart is doing that, and he might have opinions about sexuality, I am with the MIT, the murder squad, and I couldn't care less. What consenting adults do isn't part of my mandate, so long as everyone stays on the right side of the line. That's why I'm here...'

'What have you heard?'

'Not much. But we have heard that you're not just a member, more of the leader.'

'Someone's got to, otherwise it'd never happen. When you get to our age, pal, people need to plan ahead. Babysitters, all that jazz. And the excuses in times like this don't come so easily. Can't be playing squash or meeting the same pal in Berwick, you know?'

'I can imagine. I hear you've got a private group on Schoolbook.'

'Right. And I'm not naming names. It's all secret. We don't use real names.'

'Understandable, sir. Are they locals?'

'Aye. From Dalkeith down to Gala. I post about a meet-up, where and when, then they say whether they're coming along or not. We've got codewords, safewords, all that jazz.'

'And how do you know you won't get disturbed?'

'We kind of don't? That's all part of the fun. Had a couple join in at one in November.'

'Wasn't that a bit cold?'

'We all warmed ourselves up nicely.'

Cullen didn't have to wonder what form that took. 'Listen, my role here isn't to run this contact tracing, okay? Someone found a dead body this morning in Gore Glen. Probably been there since Friday night. Anything you can give us that might help, it'd be appreciated.'

'Male or female?'

'Female. Forties. Dyed blonde hair. And I can't help you with a photo. Sorry.'

'Well, the thing is, a lot of the women wear masks, so it's not like it'll be much of a help.'

'But if you gave me access to this Schoolbook group?'

'No chance. That's confidential. Secret. I'd be betraying a lot of trust.'

Worse than the masons, though hopefully with fewer serving officers. 'I understand your difficulty, sir, but we've got an unidentified dead body. Someone's wife or daughter or mother.'

'Sorry. I can't help.'

'Well, there was a woman there, wearing a mask. We need to speak to her.'

'A mask?'

Cullen tapped his own one. 'Not one like this. A sex mask. Like that Tom Cruise film, *Eyes Wide Shut*.'

'Can't help you, pal.'

'No, you can.' Cullen picked up a sleeping silver laptop. 'You're going to show me the list of your members here. Might be some clue.'

Leonard's eyes shifted around the room. He looked trapped, but was out of diversions. 'Fine.' He grabbed the machine and swivelled it round.

Cullen had to break the two metre guidelines as he made sure he didn't wipe the bloody thing.

But no, Leonard behaved himself. He opened the infernal Schoolbook site, and navigated to the Forums section, and Midlothian Rambling Club. A load of messages in the middle, and members down the right side.

Cullen snatched the machine out of his grasp and scanned through the photos. The profile name was Izzy Wizzy Let's Get Bizzy. A sexy black-and-white photo of a woman's shoulder, with "Good Girl" tattooed on the join with her arm.

Christ, it was Isobel Geddes.

10

Sometimes all you can do is whistle, know what I mean?

This place... Man. Wedale House, a big old manse, wedged between the road and the kirk. Three storeys with some of that mock Tudor stuff, but not too tacky, and a sprawling ground floor with one of those fancy new extensions like what we had put in to ours. Adds a ton of extra space, and choosing it all yourself? Magic.

So I give it the old whistle. 'And I thought her *pomme de terre* in Porty was fancy.'

Shepherd frowns at us as he presses the buzzer. 'You mean *pied-à-terre*.'

'Don't put words in my mouth, Lukey-boy.'

'*Pomme de terre* means potato. *Pied-à-terre* is what you were reaching for.'

'I know precisely what I meant. It's called a joke, you goat.'

'Brian, don't call me a goat.'

'Sorry, Sarge.' I stab the buzzer and something clangs inside the house, like the bell's broken. 'Think she's actually in?'

'We'll see.' Shepherd looks back down the lane towards his flash motor. Bit fancy for a DS to drive, but man alive, was it a smooth ride. Have to see about getting myself one with the old boy's dosh. Thing about having a wee baby girl, rather than a total dickhead of a son, is that I want the world to be a better place for her. Having an electric car rather than spewing out petrol fumes, that's got to be doing my bit, isn't it?

Buxton and Hunter are hanging around it, inspecting it like a pair of yokels who've discovered a rocket ship on their farm.

'Trouble is,' Shepherd rasps the designer stubble on his chin, 'I grew up round here. Melrose, mind, but I went to school with people who lived in this area. Keep themselves to themselves, you know?'

'I know the area well, Luke my man. The ex-wife's from here.'

'Didn't know that.'

She's not, but see winding up this chump? Too easy... 'This place used to be a restaurant or something, didn't it?'

'It was a successful B&B, aye. Had a decent bar. Got my first pint in there.'

'Underage?'

'No comment.' Shepherd's trying the buzzer again. One of those things where we'll take turns to keep pressing it and pressing it to see who's the most alpha, and Shepherd's going to lose. 'The previous lot had to sell due to the financial crisis. Isobel Geddes and her husband got it for a song.'

'How's she manage to afford this and the place in Porty?'

'We should've asked her ex.'

That snidey lanky buggerhead. 'Wonder where he stays. Holyrood Palace?'

Shepherd actually laughs at that. 'Maybe.' He grabs the handle and the door opens. 'Well, well, well. Given that our last intelligence on the missing person is that she was seen here on Friday, then we've got no choice but to enter. Correct?'

'Couldn't have said it better myself, Luke, my man.'

Shepherd waves at the pair of wankers inspecting his motor, until Buxton notices, then he thumbs inside and leads me on through into a courtyard. Enough spaces for a whole fleet of cars, but there's just a handyman's van there. Very strange. No signage on the thing, but it's manky and someone's written "GOD BLESS" in the dirt. Even stranger.

The garden's pretty lush, have to say. Cottage garden vibe,

with a lawn big enough to play not just croquet but at least nine holes of golf on. Surrounded by beds of flowers.

Lovely place. Maybe I should buy this when the old man's cash comes in?

Shepherd peers in the window. 'You haven't been acting yourself, Brian.'

'How so?'

'Well, you've not been swearing. When we met all those years ago, it was eff this and eff that.'

'Well, Luke, I'm a reformed character.'

'Believe that when I see it.' Shepherd walks over to the house. 'Bizarre.' He tries the handle and the door slides open. 'Make sure this is going in your notebook, okay? I don't want any malarkey.'

'You expecting a dead body?'

'I don't expect anything, Brian.' Shepherd snaps on some gloves, then tightens his mask. 'Simon, Craig, can you boys take the upstairs?'

Buxton is talking to someone on the blower, hopefully running the plates for the work van. 'Be with you in a minute, sarge.'

'Sure thing.' Shepherd steps into the hall.

I follow him in and it's like I've walked into one of Apinya's interior magazines. The place is immaculate, like it's barely been lived in after extensive redecoration. Ready to move in, even with the nice furniture.

'You wanting to split up while we search, Luke?'

'Not so fast. When I said no malarkey, I mean it. We're doing it room by room, okay?' Shepherd beckons us into the kitchen. 'You take that half, I'll take this.' He looks round just in time to see Tweedle Dumb and Tweedle Monster Ding-Dong heading up the stairs like a pair of good boys.

Christ, they were never this good with me.

I mean, there's a big cupboard and that takes ten seconds to walk over, open the door and confirm no human being inside. Coffee machine looks fancy. Could do with a wee cup, have to say. Fridge is a bit sticky, one of those big American things, but when I open it, I'm a bit disappointed that it's not filled with human remains. 'It's good having you with us, Luke.'

Shepherd's opened a door to a big walk-in cupboard. 'How come?'

'Well, the way Cullen works it, he's got three female DSs. Chantal Jain, Lauren Reid and Angela Caldwell.'

'Wait. *Caldwell's* a DS?'

'Acting. And I think it's only because Methven wouldn't let Cullen promote Craig Hunter.'

'With good reason.'

'Oh?'

Shepherd sighs at us. 'I know Hunter of old. He's a good constable, but he's not a sergeant. And with you, Craig and the English lad, I seem to have inherited a bit of a sausage fest.'

'Speaking of sausage, you should see what Buxton is packing.'

Shepherd stares at us. 'Anyway, I don't see why three female sergeants is an issue.'

'Well, don't you think it's a bit much?'

'You wouldn't say that about three male sergeants.'

Boy thinks he has a point. 'Aye, but that's always been the case.'

He looks over at us. 'I actually laud Cullen for it. It's the way of the future. Restorative promotions.'

'Sounds a bit *woke* to me.'

'You might not be swearing, Brian, but you haven't changed your spots, have you?'

Cheeky sod.

Aside from the absence of human remains, the fridge has been stocked up, and from that Markies food hall down in Gala, I'd wager. Nice stuff, but all of it from the deals, and nothing that healthy. Weird how it looks like nothing's been taken, though. Three for seven quid on most of it, right? Well, all three are here. Two massive pizzas too. And a meal deal for the Chinese stuff. Curious.

'When I met you ten years ago, you were a DI, now you're a DC. That must hurt.' Shepherd's deep inside that cupboard now. 'Way I hear it, Brian, is that you lost out.'

'Got to be philosophical about these things, Luke. I'm over it, believe me. Just biding my time.'

'I find that hard to believe.'

'Seriously. I'm done. Just waiting, then I'll be gone. Won't see me for dust.' But this boy's just come out of his tenure in the Complaints, so he might have an inside track on a few things. 'Heard there's people interested in Cullen.'

'People?'

'Investigation-y people. Anything in it?'

'There's always a tale behind a meteoric rise like Scott's, isn't there?'

Oh aye? Is this boy actually investigating him? Maybe he still is Complaints. That Secret Rozzer podcast is spilling all sorts of beans. Stands to reason they'd home in on Cullen, but so quickly? Well, well.

'Not aware of any dirt *per se*, Luke. You got any juice?'

Something thuds in Shepherd's cupboard. 'What have we here?'

I give up checking the fridge and wander over. Wish that hadn't happened. Love a bit of gossip, me.

Shepherd's standing by a locked door. 'Rest of the house sounds empty, but this is locked. Doesn't that strike you as a bit odd?'

'Extremely.' I've got my phone out and am calling Buxton. 'Here, King Dong, you boys got anything upstairs?'

'Two rooms down, nothing so far.'

'Rightio.' I end the call. 'What do you think?'

'We need to get through there.'

So I give him a wide grin. 'Use the force, Luke.'

Shepherd stares hard at us. Poor sap's probably heard that a million times. Well, tough. 'Stand back.'

'You're going to batter it down?'

'I've searched for a key. Nothing. If she's down there, we might be able to save her life.'

I doubt she's anywhere near here, of course. Trouble with cops like Shepherd is they've got a hero complex like you wouldn't believe. Always have to be the knight in shining armour.

He lashes out with his foot and there's a deep thud as the door swings open.

'Thought you were going to use a bit of shoulder?'

'That's for idiots.' Shepherd enters the door and turns on a light.

I follow him in. Steps leading down. 'Oooh, shiny.'

'Shut up.' Shepherd's already halfway down.

None of the fancy paint and wallpaper of the rest of the house down here, just bare stone walls and wooden steps. It opens out into a big vaulted place, probably where the minister used to keep his sex slaves or something.

'Reminds me a bit of when we had this swedge down under the Old Town in Edinburgh. That was spooky. Almost died!'

But all Isobel Geddes has is boxes and boxes of stuff. Saves on storage, I guess.

'You take that one.' Before I can get a word in edgeways, Shepherd's casing out the boxes down one aisle.

So I head down mine, like a good wee soldier.

There's a strange grunting, and I don't think it's Shepherd trying to form a coherent thought.

Something rattles. Metal. Loud. Sounds like a cage, maybe?

Christ, is she tied up down here?

I speed up, but have to stop dead. There's a cable running across the flagstones, a right trip hazard and no mistaking. I follow it to the wall, then the other way to a pile of storage boxes.

And the source of the moaning is under a big blue sheet.

I shake it off.

A man is tied up in a cage, naked as the day he was born. Looks like crocodile clips are attached to his old fella, connected to the mains.

His eyes open and he looks right at me. Whatever he's trying to say, the black knickers stuffed into his mouth are blocking it.

11

Cullen followed McKeown and Elvis's squad car through Stow, a long row of cottages on both sides of the main road at a couple of points. Surrounded by big hills, wooded to the left, bare to the right. A train trundled south, and he had no idea that they were still running, but then again even frontline workers needed public transport.

And he had no idea how to pronounce the village's name. St-oh? St-ow? Maybe there was some weird third way he couldn't fathom. Village names could be like that, especially down here in the Borders.

Elvis's indicator flicked on and Cullen parked behind him. Seemed to be a few cars parked up, just a hundred metres or so from the national speed limit signs heading south, and the "Thanks for driving carefully!" message, like it was an invitation to drive like an idiot now. He checked his phone for messages and missed calls.

Evie was front and centre:

NEVER. AGAIN.

Then another one with a selfie of her on the sofa, with two sleeping boys either side.

Maybe again.

Cullen tapped back a reply. *Looks like you're having more fun than me. Sorry about this.* He locked his phone, just as a notification flashed up and the screen went black. He tapped the screen and saw it.

Another episode of the Secret Rozzer.

And he got that tightness in his neck, like the tendons were about to snap.

Without thinking, he was out of the car and opening the other car's driver door.

Elvis was tapping away on his phone.

Cullen grabbed his shoulder and pinned him into the seat.

Elvis jerked forward and smacked his knees off the wheel. 'Aya!'

'Get out.' Cullen pulled him out onto the road, just as a car whizzed past, way too fast for a village road. He nodded at McKeown. 'Go and see the lay of the land.'

'Sir.' McKeown buttoned up his coat as he sloped off.

Cullen held out his phone to Elvis. 'Paul, is this you?'

'Is what?'

Cullen shoved the phone into his face. 'This podcast!'

'Eh? Of course not.' But Elvis couldn't look at him. Kept looking everywhere but at Cullen, especially at the phone screen. 'And that looks like a correction to the previous episode.'

Cullen checked it, and maybe Elvis was right. He couldn't remember the number of the last one, but it might be the same. 'Have you been listening to it?'

'Aye, it's cracking stuff. Gripping, as they say.'

'Paul, if this is you and you keep denying it, so help me but I'll—'

'How can it be?! I've been with you all the time!'

'No, you were at the CCTV office while I was with DS Murray in Pathhead. And besides, you could've scheduled it in advance.'

'Seriously, Scott, it's not me.'

'Is it Bain?'

'I don't know.'

'You two were doing that beer podcast together. That trip to America?'

'Aye, *were*.' Elvis snorted. 'Look, all that crap in America has kind of soured me on him, if I'm being honest.'

Maybe Cullen was barking up the wrong tree here. Thing with Elvis was, he was always that bit too cool for school, always hiding some big part of himself away. Never knew if you were speaking to Elvis, or to the true Paul Gordon.

Cullen pocketed his phone and zapped his car's central locking. 'Is this the—'

'Why don't you ask Bain? He's right there.'

Cullen looked over and, sure enough, Bain and Buxton were halfway down a lane, laughing and patting each other on the back. McKeown was joining in but had the look of someone who didn't get the joke but wanted to be friends anyway.

A strange grouping if Cullen had ever seen one. He set off up the winding lane towards them. 'What are you doing here?'

Buxton looked round with a frown. 'Scott, mate, you gotta see it for yourself.' He thumbed towards a tall manse house.

Wedale House, the address they were heading for.

'What are you doing here?'

'What do you think?' Bain coughed into his hand, but he was still laughing. His face and head were completely smooth these days, which made him seem even creepier than usual. 'Looking for that missing MSP.'

'She lives here?'

'Aye, that's what I said. She's not in, mind.'

Cullen got that thudding in his neck again. Wouldn't be the first time two cases found themselves merging. A missing woman in Edinburgh, and a found body in Midlothian. Didn't take the world's best detective to link them. Maybe it was the after-effects of this bug, but he was definitely not on his A-game.

He'd asked Shepherd to keep an eye open, but the sod hadn't kept him informed.

'What are you finding so funny?'

Bain was struggling to keep a straight face. 'Go into the basement. Through the kitchen. You'll see.'

Pair of idiots.

CULLEN FOUND THE KITCHEN, though with a house that size, it wasn't uncommon to have more than one.

He stormed across the courtyard. His phone rang, blaring out "Mr Brightside" by The Killers.

Deeley calling...

Cullen answered. 'Hey, what's up?'

One of those long whistling sighs. 'Well, Young Skywalker, I managed to squeeze in a wee look at your victim. Don't thank me, but strangulation is definitely your cause of death. And the victim definitely had old bruises. Some were two weeks' old, judging by the fading.'

'So she had previous?'

'And then some.' Cullen had a flash of Isobel Geddes in the morning's paper, always wearing a scarf. Always.

She was their victim.

'Cheers, Jimmy.' He killed the call and listened hard.

Someone was rattling something, and very loudly and very far away.

Cullen walked into a larder, then through an open door to a set of stairs heading down. The place was dark and barely lit, and the rattling was getting louder and closer.

The place was rammed with storage boxes, two aisles passing between them. The rattling seemed to be coming from the second one.

There was a smell of excrement.

Shepherd was halfway down, on his knees. 'Stay still!'

A loud scream tore out. 'Get off me!' A man's voice.

'I need to get you—' Shepherd noticed Cullen walking over and stopped whatever he was doing. 'Scott?'

'Luke.' Cullen got a better look at the scene.

A large animal cage sat there, partially covered with a blue sheet. Inside, a naked man was wriggling and writhing. His buttocks were smeared brown.

Cullen almost gagged. 'Luke, what the hell is—'

'Scott, help me!' Shepherd was covered in shit himself, all

over his suit and shirt and shoes. 'I'm trying to free this idiot, but he's fighting me.'

Cullen didn't want to get too close. Whatever the hell was going on here, though, this man looked like the only lead in two cases. Two cases that were getting weirder by the second.

Shepherd reached in and grabbed the manacles around the man's neck.

He got punched in the forearm for his troubles.

Rattling metal and footsteps came from behind him. 'Out of the way!'

Shepherd stepped away and let two paramedics past. 'He'll need to be sedated.'

Cullen stood there, taking it in, trying to formulate a strategy. The man was tied up, looking dehydrated and hungry from the dryness around his mouth. He was big, though, at least six-five, and with heavy muscles.

Wait a second...

Through the smeared shit, Cullen could make out a tattoo of Tracy Chapman.

'Rob?'

The monster in the cage stopped his wriggling and looked over at Cullen. 'Scotty?'

Christ, it *was* him. Big Rob. Robert Woodhead, AKA Rob Szczepański. Cullen's favourite knucklehead bodybuilder. He was massive ten years ago, but he'd almost doubled in size since.

'What the hell are you doing here, Rob?'

'I'm fine, Scotty.' Rob stood up, hands palms out. 'I'm fine.' But a chain jerked him back and he slipped over in his cage.

'I need to get out of here.' Shepherd squelched off through the basement towards the stairs.

Cullen stayed there. 'You really okay, Rob?'

'Does it look it?'

A paramedic was reaching a gloved hand in to the cage. 'You know where there's a key, son?'

'Not allowed to know.'

'You what?'

'She keeps it from me.'

Cullen got it, right there and then. His missing person and murder victim were now also linked to a sexual deviant in a basement. And someone he knew. 'Was it Isobel?'

Big Rob looked over at him. 'Aye.'

'Right.' Cullen stood up and let the paramedics get at him. 'You get him hydrated and stabilised, I'll try and find the key.'

∼

THE FRESH AIR never tasted as sweet, but Cullen couldn't clear the smell of shit.

Still, he didn't have to look too far for his team.

Shepherd was the centre of a huddle by the main road, looking fed up and pissed off, huddled under a paramedic's blanket.

Bain was leading the laughter. 'Might need to change your togs, sarge.'

Shepherd narrowed his eyes at Bain. 'Mind if I take your car?'

'Aye, I do, as it happens.'

'Well, you're driving me.' Shepherd clicked his fingers. 'Now!'

Cullen got Bain's attention. 'Give us a second. And see if anyone's found a key for that cage.' He followed Shepherd over to his car. 'Luke, sorry I haven't had a chance to catch up. Been flat out on a murder case.'

'Aye, aye. I get it, Scott.' Shepherd laughed. 'Christ, this is *minging*. I'll have to burn it.'

'You going to head home?'

'Nah, it'll take ages to get to Edinburgh and back. Besides, the rate I go through them, I get my suits from Tesco. Cheap as hell and easily replaced when you run through the knees twice a month. I'll get that idiot Bain to buy me one from Gala. I can get a shower in the nick there.' His nostrils twitched. 'Not that it'll get this stink out.'

'You were doing a good thing, Luke.'

'Wasn't worth it. I got covered in shite, and it turns out you knew the guy.'

'Strangest thing. Me and Craig met him ten years ago on a stupid case at a gym.'

'Christ, I remember that.' Shepherd smirked. 'Seems like yesterday.'

Cullen sighed. 'How you doing?'

'Aside from being covered in shite? I'm okay, Scott. Okay. And okay is good when you work for Police Scotland.'

'Isn't it just?' Cullen folded his arms. 'Okay, so I've got to wrap my arms around both these cases. When Methven took them on, they were separate, but now... A missing MSP seems to be the body in the woods. Or at least, she was nearby while the victim was killed.'

'Gore Glen, eh?'

'You know it?'

Shepherd nodded. 'Did a stint in Gorebridge about, ooh, fifteen years ago. That glen is bonkers. If it wasn't underage kids drinking and fighting, it was overage kids drinking and shagging. Weird place, and then some.'

'Takes all sorts, eh?' Cullen moved to clap his shoulder, but pulled back. 'Welcome back from the Complaints, though.'

Something dark passed over Shepherd's eyes, like there were a million thoughts he wasn't sharing. Or couldn't share. 'Did my three years and now I'm back to Gen Pop, as they say.'

'Luke, you get yourself—'

'Scott.' Murray charged past them, giving the thumbs up. 'Here it is.'

A burly fireman stood next to him, clutching a pair of bolt cutters. The guy had the look of one of those calendars. 'You're sure?'

Murray stopped. 'No, now you mention it, we found a key in a bag that perfectly fits these manacles.'

The fireman raised his eyebrows. 'You an expert?'

'No, I'm joking.' Murray frowned at him, like he was wondering who the hell he was. 'Yes, I'm sure.' He stood back and watched him snap away, then nudged Cullen. 'Remember that young Eva Law I used to work with?'

'She's in my team.' Cullen was aware of McKeown looking their way. No idea what he was doing here. Maybe he was supposed to give Cullen an update? He couldn't remember. 'What about her?'

'She knows her way around a lot of esoteric sexual equipment, apparently.'

The one problem Cullen hadn't been able to shift. Eva Law. Why she was still hanging around, he had no idea. 'Okay, can you get them to ... clean up Rob and take him over to Lauder police station for interview?'

'Sure thing.' Murray winked at him. 'But don't forget the alarm code.'

Shepherd tilted his head at them. 'Eh?'

Murray smirked. 'Few years ago, Cullen set off the alarm when we had to meet a witness in there. Place is closed to the public, so some poor bugger had to come up from Gala to switch it off.'

Shepherd nodded. 'Sounds like Scott Cullen to me.'

'Catch you later.' Murray set off at double speed.

Cullen gave him the nod. 'I'll let you get yourself sorted out, Luke. See you over there.' He walked down to the street, wanting to check his phone for messages.

A blue Mondeo pulled up and Cullen didn't even have to check who was inside to just *know* who it was. Pair of bastards.

Rich McAlpine was first out of the passenger side and clocked Cullen straight away. His hair had grown out quite a bit, and it didn't suit him. Not much did. 'Scott.'

Alan Lyall sat behind the wheel, taking his time getting out, maybe wanting to relish the frosty reunion between them. He was a whole other kettle of arsehole.

Why were two *Argus* journalists here so quickly?

'Rich.' Cullen put his phone away. He wanted to cross the road, but there was an unexpected convoy of tractors heading their way.

By the time it passed, Rich was on the phone to someone, but Alan was out of the car. 'Vicky sends her love, Scott.'

'Bet she sends you her hate, though.' Cullen stuffed his hands in his pockets. So much history with these two idiots. And he needed to stop them getting anywhere near the story, which was bound to be impossible. 'Out for a nice walk in the borders, are we? Get your daily exercise in?'

'Something like that.'

'Strange how you're parking here, Alan. Of all places.'

'Well, you know how it is, Scott. See an old lover's friend, and you just have to say hi.'

'Why are you really here?'

'See, Scotty, Vicks wouldn't be as daft as you. She would keep pricks like me and Rich at arm's reach. Probably bust our balls.' Alan laughed. 'She certainly wouldn't send two cops out to speak to us about spiking a story.'

Shepherd and Bain, no doubt. That would come back to bite Cullen on the arse. And soon. 'Alan, as far as I was aware, the pressure to spike the story wasn't from us. We were checking why *you* spiked it. And then why you decided to run it.'

'And you didn't think we'd come down here to see what's what?' Alan shook his head. 'Must think we're a pair of daft bastards.'

'You're getting nothing out of us.'

'Oh, Scott, you're like an open book, mate.' Alan folded his arm. 'You tracked down Isobel's lover?'

'Her lover?'

'Aye. Young-ish guy, built like a tank. No, three tanks stuck end-to-end. He's *massive*. No idea who he is, mind.'

'Shame.'

'Scott, I'm giving you solid info here. Least you could do is return the favour.'

'No way.'

Alan gave him a hard look, then glanced over at Rich. 'That's disappointing.'

'I'm not disappointed.' Cullen felt his mobile thrum in his pocket. He checked it. A text from Methven:

At Lauder. Get over here now.

He looked round, ready to attack Alan again, but the Mondeo was already driving off, heading south towards Galashiels. Looked like they were following Shepherd and Bain. No doubt there would be a story in the morning's paper about two of Police Scotland's finest burning some clothes in the Borders...

~

LAUDER NICK WAS A STRANGE PLACE, a modern-ish building stuck next to a much more recent housing development on the town's southern tip. Well, what used to be it, as it stretched another half a mile south on the A68.

Cullen got out of his car onto the street. A blast of horn came from the parking bay a few over.

Methven's Range Rover tore into the world's worst parallel park.

Cullen's grin was torn off his face when he saw who was in the passenger seat.

DI Ally Davenport, his old boss. Great. 'Scott, Scott, Scott.' He thrust out a fist, ready to be bumped. 'How the devil are you, my man?'

'Okay, Ally. Okay.'

'Long time, no see.'

Cullen shrugged. 'Been busy.'

'Last I saw you, Scott, you were a green-around-the-gills Acting DC. Now look at you. Methven's little prince.'

'Almost ten years, Ally. Lot can happen in that time.'

'Sure can. And now you're a peer. Very, very strange.' Davenport looked back the way, but Methven was still in his car, fussing over his phone. 'Spoken to Luke Shepherd, and he says you know this Big Rob guy?'

'You do too, Ally. That case in Rock Hard Gym.'

'Christ. That takes me back. Bloody hell. That was him?'

'No, he just happened to be there at the time.'

'Well, you should be leading the interview, Scott, if you've already built the rapport.'

'Craig knows him too.'

'Craig Hunter? Christ... He still around?'

'Why wouldn't he be?'

'No reason.'

'Ally, I'll have a team meeting to discuss the interview strategy once Hunter and Bain—'

'*Bain?*' Davenport's mouth hung open. 'Thought he was in Glasgow?'

'That was years ago. He's a DC now.'

'Well, a scumbag like that still being a cop really gets my goat. Only time I dealt with him, he was out of control. You worked for him, didn't you? How could you cope with that?'

Cullen wanted to defend Bain, to say that he wasn't as bad as all that. But the truth was, he was as bad as all that, and worse. And it wasn't like he had some redeeming qualities, he'd just managed to solve a few cases recently. Either blind luck or just experience. And Cullen had chucked away more than one opportunity to bin him.

No, Cullen needed a different tack. 'Sometimes people learn *because of*, sometimes people learn *in spite of...* You're jealous that I chose him over you, aren't you?'

'Aye, good one.' Davenport laughed. 'Any idea where Shepherd is?'

'Had a slight wardrobe malfunction.'

'Sounds like something I really don't want to know.' Davenport folded his arms. 'Scott, whatever. Craig can interview Rob, but I'd like it to be under Shepherd's supervision. Okay?'

Cullen still hated feeling subordinate to him. He might have a longer record, but they were the same grade. 'That was my plan all along.'

12

Christ, it still stinks of shite in here.

The root of all the ming is this Rob Woodhead boy. It's like when I went to one of my boy's parents' nights when he was in primary and you see all these tiny wee chairs. He's like that, but these are adult chairs.

I remember him from that case a few years back, where Cullen thought he was a vigilante. Nonsense, of course. No way this boy could hurt anything, he's way too big and slow. I mean, sure, if he connects you're gonna know all about it, but that's a very big if.

Must be steroids. Meaning his wanger must be miniscule. Bless him.

Hunter's a big lad too, but nothing on the scale of him. 'So why were you down in that dungeon?'

Rob laughs. 'A dungeon, eh? Oh you cheeky so-and-so. Craig, mate. It's a complex matter.'

'And you're a complex man, Rob. How about you try and tell me how it got so complicated?'

'It's a bit embarrassing, isn't it?'

'Sharing is caring, Rob. Sure you've got a tattoo to that effect.'

'Aye.' He laughs at Hunter's patter. 'On my thigh. Good memory.'

'Hard to scratch it off my cerebellum, isn't it?' Hunter splays his paws on the table. Bloody things are covered in scar tissue around the joints. Christ knows what he's been up to.

God, this is getting us nowhere.

Hunter's supposed to have this rapport with the lad. Even sat in here with the big lump while I drove that clown to Gala Tesco's and bought him a new suit. Picked the most stupid one they had, of course. Beige. I mean, Shepherd looks like he's on safari now. But whatever Hunter thinks he's got with this boy, he clearly hasn't. There's rapport and there's talking shite to a fanny in the gym.

Sod it.

I lean over the table. 'Here, Rob. Must be pretty emasculating for you.'

'What must?'

'Being tied up like that.'

'Don't know what you mean.'

'Well, I assume this is some kink you've got? Get tied up and left for hours. Cheeky wee bit of high jinks, right? Problem is, you couldn't free yourself.'

'Listen, I'm thankful you guys arrived when you did.'

'Thankful, eh?' I sit there, nodding. 'Right. So, I'm going to put my cards on the table, Rob. You're a straight-talking guy. I'm the same. Way I see it, you're into some kinky stuff with Isobel. I'm not judging you. Consenting adults and all that. Trouble is, Isobel's missing.'

He's frowning at us. 'What?'

'Didn't turn up at her work today. Further complicated by the paper running a story about her this morning.'

Boy looks away and scratches his Desperate Dan chin. 'She knew they were onto her a few weeks ago.'

'And it didn't stop her?'

'Nope. She figured she was damned anyway, so...' Rob shrugs. 'Just got on with it.'

'Now.' I hold up a finger. 'Most people would start to think she'd run away from all her trouble and strife.'

'Aye?'

'Thing is, Rob.' I pretend to tug at something round my neck. 'The manacles you were tied up with, they were locked.'

Boy knows he's gubbed here. Can't make eye contact. 'Right.'

'Now's the time, son. You talk, we listen.'

He looks right at us. 'What do you want to know?'

'When was the last time you saw Isobel?'

He gives the deepest sigh in the world. 'I haven't seen her since she tied me up on Friday night.'

'So three days ago?'

'*Three days?*'

'Son, it's Monday lunchtime.'

'Christ. I could've *died* in that cage! Holy fuck!' He's shaking his head. 'This was her game, okay? Playing me, edging me, building up the teasing until I can't handle it any more, then the sex would be like two wild animals.'

'Only you were covered in your own shite.'

'Aye. That's not her thing. She'd have hosed me down, good and proper.'

'So where was she going when she tied you up?'

Rob stares at the ceiling. Looking at me and Hunter must seem like the worst thing ever. Seeing that shame and anger and fear in his eyes. 'You just told me you found her purse.'

'Need to hear it from you.'

'She was going to Gore Glen.'

'Not for a walk, I presume?'

'No, it was ... She'd told me all about it. She was going to what she called a gathering. You'd call it dogging. She was going to watch a cleaner get her back doors smashed in by a builder and a bus driver in the woods, then she was going to come back and let me go.'

'That turn you on?'

'A bit.' He shakes his head again, like he's denying it even to himself. 'Maybe more than a bit.'

'So you weren't at Gore Glen?'

'No, she didn't let me go.'

'This a long-term thing between you?'

'It's not love, if that's what you mean.'

'So you're just letting her put you in a cage?'

'I'm a filthy animal. Why are you interested?'

'Because Isobel's dead.'

Big Rob nods. Guy like that, emotions are hard to feel, let alone process. Everything is handled by a quip or a barb or a joke. Except for the rage he'd get from those 'roids. Lucky Hunter's here with all his Bruce Lee stuff.

But Big Rob clearly does feel it, right in his heart. And I would know, I'm exactly the same. Deep down, the pain is so raw you just don't know what to do with it.

He looks right at us through damp eyes. 'When did this happen?'

'Friday night.'

'Huh. That explains it.'

And maybe I'm wrong. Maybe he just doesn't care. Maybe he's a sociopath who can only feel emotions when someone shoves him in a cage and treats him like a dog.

'You didn't kill her, did you?'

'I was in a cage!'

'We found you in a cage on Monday. We have no way of establishing whether you were in that cage on Friday night, or you just locked yourself away ten minutes before we found you.'

'What about the key?'

'Aye, they never make more than one for these things, do they?'

'I was covered in my own shit!'

I shake my head at the boy, show him I'm denying him his truth. 'Let's just go with you not killing her. Can you think of anyone who might have?'

'Nope.'

'What about this bus driver or builder up at the glen?'

'They don't know who she is.'

'Oh?'

'She wears a mask there. Even naked.'

'Powerful woman like that. Got to make you wonder what she'd see in a boy like you.'

'It's because I'm the opposite of her ex-husband. He's a needledick top.'

'And you're a bottom?'

Big Rob shrugs.

'And you're not a needledick, eh?'

'That's my business.'

I end the recording, then sit back and fold my arms. 'Know this boy, cock like a stallion. Should see it, man.'

Rob's lips twist up. Managed to get through to him now. He is actually disgusted by this chat.

But not as much as Hunter. Arsehole grabs my arm and Christ it hurts. 'Stop.' His whisper is a hiss, but he lets go and leans over the table and restarts the recording. 'Rob, remember back in the day, when me and Scotty used to work out with you at that gym?'

'Rock Hard. Right?'

'Right. Not there any more. You go to Ultraman now?'

'Well, I did. Lockdown's buggered it all up. Got a bar at home and some kick-ass weights. Saves me a packet. Why you asking?'

'Well, you weren't exactly backwards in coming forwards, were you? Thought you were definitely a giver.'

'Ach, that's all stories for the locker room, Craig. I had a kink. And it's grown, big style.'

'Being tied up?'

'And then some. See, when I work out or I'm out cutting trees.' Boy looks right at us. 'I'm a tree surgeon.' Then back at Hunter. 'I'm doing it all, working away. And I have this need to be taken care of. Not so much looked after as absolutely dominated.'

'And that's Isobel?'

'Right.'

I pick up my tea ready for a sip. 'How did you meet her?'

'Moved to Stow a year back, trying to get closer to nature, you know? Hills here are great for walking, and the mountain biking trails? Amazing. Anyway, one day I'm picking my boy up from school.'

Almost spray my tea over the boy. 'You've got a *kid*?'

'Four of them. My youngest two aren't even at primary. Oldest is at university.'

Well bugger me with a tree trunk. This boy has lived a life. 'Are you married?'

'Not *married* married, but I live with someone. Sure.'

'She's not going to be worried about your whereabouts?'

'We have an understanding. She went away to Corfu last November with the girls, got absolutely smashed in by these rugby lads.' He snarls. 'Anyway, I was going to pick up my boy from school, and I take the long way round. Strap on two twenty-eight kilo kettlebells and walk up the hills. Best way to burn fat and lose hydration. Supposed to be doing some photos for a magazine next week.'

'A porno?'

He scowls at us. 'Get your mind out of the gutter. No, it's called *Bold and Beautiful*.'

'Which are you?'

'Both. So I'm running up the hill out of the village on the Earlston road, then I clear the last houses, go round the bend and I see a car's broken down. Foxy lady like that, couldn't help myself. I used to work as a mechanic, so I got her back up and running.'

'And you say you're a tree surgeon now?'

'Aye. So she thanked me by taking me out for a meal in Melrose. At a hotel. Where she'd booked a room upstairs too. It wasn't an Indian, but things ended up getting pretty spicy.'

'Quite like being treated like that?'

'Way of the world now, my friend. Equality has a lot of opportunities for boys like me.'

'And this became a thing, then?'

'Oh, aye. Isobel's ex wasn't really into getting tied up and all that. And she liked to take charge. And she preferred a bigger man. I'm so strong that I could carry her while we... While we made love. She loved it.'

'This is all very entertaining, son, and I can see there's a deep connection there. But did she ever talk about her job?'

'Strictly verboten.'

But I'm clutching at straws here. Plastic ones too, not

organic natural ones. This boy might just be her Dick On Legs, just some vessel for her depravations, and he's not the sharpest tool in the box, either, so I'll clutch those straws and see if there's any long ones left. 'You got any idea who might want her dead?'

'Search me.'

Just what this filthy pervert wants, isn't it? My stubby wee fingers all over him. 'Look, I'll be honest with you here, son. We're struggling a bit. Last we know of Isobel is she might've been at this dogging thing at Gore Glen. You ever go to one?'

'Nope.'

'She ever talk about the people who did?'

'No.'

'What about the bus driver, the cleaner—'

'They're all made up. Listen, this one time, Isobel made me have a foursome with this freaky couple at their house in Gorebridge.'

13

Cullen carried his coffee cup and led Buxton down the short corridor in Gorebridge police station. The pale walls were splashed with tea and coffee stains. Somehow. And the place still had that strange cheesy smell, like someone had caught athlete's foot years ago and passed it on to all their colleagues. 'You let Big Rob go?'

'Yeah.' Buxton was biting down on his bottom lip with those big falsers of his. 'His work van was searched but we found nothing.'

A uniform guarded the interview room, leaning against the door jamb, checking his phone. He looked over at Cullen with bloodshot eyes. 'He's ready for you, sir.'

'Perfect, thanks.' But Cullen stayed in the corridor, sipping from his mug. Somehow the coffee from the filter machine here tasted really good, even with powdered milk. 'I feel like a bit of an idiot.'

Buxton grinned at him. 'Not like you to admit that.'

'No.' Cullen had to look away. Buxton's false teeth were starting to unsettle him. 'These were the same case. Should've seen it earlier.'

'Wise man once taught me that it's better to assume they're separate than the alternative.' Buxton slurped tea through his teeth, splashing some on the carpet tiles. 'Unpicking connections that weren't there is much harder than making them.'

'This wise man sounds like a good cop.'

'Nah, he's a dickhead.' Buxton laughed. 'It was Bain.'

'Oh God.'

'Why is he still around, Scott?'

'Si, is this you trying to explain what he's done this time?'

'Nah, it's... Never mind.'

Cullen knew there was something. And the more Buxton didn't seem to want to share it, the more he wanted to dig. 'Si, what is it?'

'Seriously, it's fine.'

Cullen also knew when to leave it like that. But he couldn't help himself. 'What's he done?'

'Joking about...' Buxton looked down at his groin '... my cock.'

'Where does he get off? Always laughing at monster ones in post mortems.'

Buxton was blushing.

Cullen decided he'd pushed it far enough. 'How are you getting on with Shepherd?'

'He's annoying but good. Got Bain in his little box. Lets him make enough of his little quips to feel useful and important, but not enough that he's got a formal complaint yet.'

'Look, Si, I won't pry, but you can always talk to me when you're ready.'

Buxton fidgeted with his teeth. 'Shepherd was asking about you.'

That made Cullen tingle in a place he didn't like tingling. 'What kind of thing?'

'Specific stuff about a case a while back.'

That didn't feel at all good.

'You know him?'

'We worked together ten years ago. I mean, I was an Acting DC with my head up my arse, and he was a DS who looked like he was going places.' He took another drink of coffee. 'Let's do this.' He carried his cup over to the door and smiled at the uniform guard. 'We'll take it from here.'

Cullen opened the interview room door and stepped in. Without looking across the table, he rested his coffee on the table and his suit jacket on the chair back.

The man sitting opposite was a beanpole who look bored, resting his head on his fist. 'I'm not saying a word without my lawyer present.'

Cullen frowned at him. 'Aren't you a lawyer?'

'Exactly, so where's my present?' He smiled broadly, then held out his hand, revealing a birthmark on his cheek, shaped like an apostrophe or a comma. 'Peter Tomlinson.'

Cullen just nodded, but it looked like Buxton was going to shake his hand, until he caught the warning glare. 'Thanks for attending, sir.'

'Not a problem.' Despite his cheery demeanour, his forehead kept on twitching. 'So, what's this about?'

Instead of asking what he plainly knew, he was playing the daft laddie, something Cullen was a master at. 'This is about your ex-wife, Mr Tomlinson.'

'I see.' A bitter smile now. 'There's still no sign of her?'

Cullen wasn't ready to give him the truth. That bomb would have to wait. 'We need to ask you a few questions about the story in the *Argus* this morning.'

'Right.' Tomlinson sat back, arms folded and looked a completely different man. Eyes narrowed, jaw clenched. 'I knew she was doing it, of course.'

'Thanks for your honesty.'

'I went round to her pied-à-terre in Portobello one Friday night to speak to her, but she wasn't in. I mean, she should've been, right?'

'And you shouldn't. We're under lockdown.'

'Right. I wasn't doing anything wrong. I live in Leith, just off the Shore, so I was doing my daily exercise. Just so happened to take me up to Porty.'

'Did you track her down?'

'The next day, I took a drive down to the Borders with my mountain bike. I mean, there was this subsequent guidance about driving for an hour, so it was all fine, right? And she was in our old home. I told her... I told her she was making a big mistake. Kept telling her to stop going, but she wouldn't listen.'

'Why is it a problem?'

'It's how it looks, isn't it? Telling everyone to stay at home, while she's driving down to stay in her second home. And her first home is much more expensive than most people's, let alone our old home in Stow. It's just not a good look. And the Borders has barely been affected by Covid, especially compared with say Greater Glasgow or Grampian. So the risk of her spreading it is colossal.'

'You seem to have been quite persistent with this, though.'

'Of course.' Tomlinson sighed. 'We, uh, we got wind that the fourth estate had got hold of it, somehow. This was on Friday. I'd been at Isobel for three weeks to stop going, but she wouldn't listen. I heard one or two of them had been staking out Wedale House, waiting for her return. Photos, you name it.'

'What did you do?'

'What anyone else would do, I tried to call in favours. A few of us did. I spent all of Saturday on the phone to the *Argus*'s senior management, trying to get the story spiked.'

'Any success?'

'It's not easy when you're dealing with a London paper, by proxy. The *Post*, they run the *Argus* like it's a section of their paper rather than...' He shook his head.

'Did you get anywhere with them?'

'I was successful. The others weren't.'

'But it was only partially successful, right?'

'Correct. I spent all of Sunday in bed, thinking I'd contracted Covid-19, but it was just food poisoning and all of the stress from Saturday. It meant I'd missed a few calls, and they went to press for the Monday edition.' He had the look of someone whose football team had conceded a last-minute equaliser, rather than anything more serious. 'I mean, I don't know why I was bothering, really. Isobel had been warned, and not just by me. And she wasn't answering anyone's calls. But this pandemic... It's important we protect the party and give a single message, isn't it?'

'When was the last time you heard from her?'

'Friday. In her office. I couldn't enter because... Well, the social distancing measures. She was obstinate. Would not listen. I stormed off, sent her an angry text, then a formal email.'

'I gather she wasn't a text, though.'

'Well, desperate times call for desperate measures.'

'Did she reply?'

Tomlinson was staring into space now. 'I didn't even get read receipts.'

Time to hit him. 'I hate to be the bearer of this news, sir.' Cullen paused, waiting for the drop, but got nothing. 'Unfortunately we found Isobel's body.'

'Oh my God.' Tomlinson crumbled into a heap. Head pressed against the table, breathing hard and heavy, moaning. 'Oh my God.'

Cullen gave him a few seconds, while he finished his coffee. He couldn't taste it now, his mouth had gone dry.

Whatever had happened between Peter Tomlinson and Isobel Geddes to make the divorce, this was hitting him hard. And while he professed to be protecting her for the sake of the party, it was all still his twisted protective instinct for her as a person, not a politician.

Cullen rested his empty cup on the table. 'We haven't confirmed that the body is Isobel. That's going to take some time, I'm afraid.'

'But you think it's her?'

'We believe it is. We found a clutch bag containing keys to her property, for instance.'

'Anything I can do, please. I want to. Need to.'

'Thanks, sir. I'll get a colleague to work with you.'

'Do you need me to identify her body?'

'Nope... did she have any identifying marks, tattoos, birthmarks, scars? A way to identify her other than her face?'

'Shit. What... What happened?'

While Tomlinson seemed genuinely distressed about this, he was still Cullen's number one suspect. 'Sir, it's important that you answer a few questions about your marriage. Is that okay?'

'Well, it's over.'

'Is it okay?'

'Fine. Sure.'

'Why did you get divorced?'

'I wish I knew.' Tomlinson ran a hand down his face. 'Isobel had a nickname, Ice-obel. She never showed her emotions. It was why she was so good at her job. You need to be able to emotionally distance yourself from the children whose futures your policies are shaping, so that you can make the sometimes-hard decisions which are for their benefit.'

It was like a switch had flipped and the grieving ex-husband had transformed into a political party lawyer.

Cullen knew he wasn't going to get much by that sort of questioning, so had to hit him hard. 'The reason wasn't this sex club, was it?'

'Sex club?'

'Don't deny it. People are speaking to us.'

'Shit.' Tomlinson sat back, snorting as he stared up at the ceiling. 'You cops, you're just sitting there having a laugh at us, aren't you? Our lives, what turns us on, it's all just a big joke to you, isn't it?'

'No, sir. It's a murder case. We need to find who murdered your ex-wife. It can often come down to why you divorced, or why you split up in the first place.'

Tomlinson shrugged, then looked right at Cullen. 'The way we talk about it, Isobel was the top. She used to dominate me. It was her thing. And everything in our marriage was her way. Everything. And I... I thought our divorce was part of it. Her controlling me, dominating me, humiliating me. And it was so *hot*. Getting kicked out like that, having to sleep in a grubby hotel. Then a better one. Then her ignoring me at work. Then getting threatening letters from lawyers. It was all so hot. But then I started to worry. We hadn't met up in months. I mean, it's a lot of set up, but when is the payoff? So I went round to talk to her, and she didn't accept our safeword. She told me it was over.'

Tomlinson looked devastated, like he was reliving the trauma again. All the pain that his brain confused with pleasure, then the lack of payoff, as he said.

Oh, he was definitely capable of murder.

But what was worse was that it was legit. Cullen would never cease to be amazed at the depravity and abuse people would wilfully submit themselves to.

'Was there anyone else?'

'Of course there was someone else. I mean, it was a sex club. We met in people's homes, or in the great outdoors, with the express goal of having group sex. But she got a lot more action than I did. It was so erotic, watching her with three men and a woman. Her eyes through that mask, only me knowing her secret, who she really was.'

'She wore a mask?'

'Right. Like in that film, the Tom Cruise one where he's ... Yeah, like that.' Tomlinson snarled. 'But that big muscle man, she saw something in him. I came home from work one day, and the doors were open. I caught him riding her on our kitchen table.'

'That must've been upsetting.'

'Deeply. Don't you see? *He* was riding *her*. I've wanted to do that for *years* but she wouldn't let me. It was all on her terms.'

'We believe that she was in Gore Glen on Friday night. Someone there may have murdered her. Or it could've been someone who wasn't there, who knew she'd be there, but who turned up to kill her.'

'What? You think I killed her?'

'Seems like you'd have a motive for her murder, sir.'

'I could never harm her! Don't you see? It's all about *her* hurting *me*!'

'So on Friday night, whe—?'

'Jesus Christ, I was at work, trying to snuff out her complete disaster! I've got twenty lawyers and senior party members who'll vouch for my whereabouts.'

Buxton sniffed. He knew where his day was going. Back to parliament to interview the great and the good, all wearing masks and socially distanced.

'But, at the heart of it all, I still love Isobel. Sometimes I tell myself we'd still be together if it wasn't for that club, but I would've found some other way to let her down.'

What a bizarre way to see the world. Or at least to derive your pleasure. 'Sir, if it's not you, who could it be?'

'The whole reason we got into that scene was when we bought our house in Stow. The previous owner made some comments, used some codewords, and well...'

'What's their name?'

14

Christ, what's this boy's name again? Used to work for Cullen, but he's not been on the scene for a wee while now. Used to be based out east, didn't he? Haddington way, maybe?

Christ! This is going to annoy me!

Anyway, this boy is standing by his pool motor in the street in Gorebridge, thumbing some shite into his phone. He looks up at us, and it's like he's seen the ghost of the Loch Ness monster. 'Bain?'

I mean, get a grip, pal!

'Aye, it's good ol' Brian Bain.' I look at Shepherd, and the lad is smirking away. Sneaky one, that. Got his cards marked. 'It's Stuart something, isn't it?'

'Christ, Brian, I hope they don't put you on the stand anymore?'

'Shut it.'

'It's Murray.' He holds out a gloved fist for Shepherd to bump through his gloves. 'DS Stuart Murray.'

'When did you—' Nope. I'm not playing that game these days. Get on with the job, do my time, then get out. Right? 'Well, Stuart, we're here to visit Ryan and Dawn Marshall. They in?'

'Aye.' Murray huffs out this big almighty sigh. 'And we're getting nowhere.'

Shepherd's turn to frown. 'Last I heard, Scott had—'

'Aye, aye. Same old story with him, though. Comes in, knocks down a few doors, then buggers off to new *shiny*. Leaving the likes of us to clear up after him. Swear, it's like having a puppy.'

Oh, there's an opening there, if I could be bothered to squeeze my way through it. 'So why are you getting nowhere?'

'Well, typical Scott Cullen, he gets his lead, finding out that Dr Isobel Geddes might've been at this dogging thing. I even found her bag for him, and let that shite-encrusted body-builder out of a cage in her basement.' He takes a deep, long breath. 'Anyway. Now Scott's in full panic mode, right? I was supposed to be here to do a bit of contact tracing about this dogging. When we came in, they were in denial about it even being a thing. Now, they're shitting themselves about whether they've passed the bug on to her parents.'

'Nightmare.' Shepherd set off up the path. 'I'll see what I can do.'

~

PLACES LIKE THIS, they all look so samey from the outside, but see inside? Totally different ball game. Mind Cullen saying something like that to us once, and the boy's right. Credit to him.

And Shepherd, he's like an Alsatian here, gnawing at this boy's legs. Figuratively, because he's sitting down, sipping on tea. 'I'm not judging you, sir. It's totally fine what you get up to.' He nods out of the window. 'DS Murray's team are aware of your situation and have arranged for tests to be conveyed to your loved ones and anyone else you might've been in close contact with. If there's a situation, we can get on top of it. And if we know they've got it, there are some steroids which might help nip it in the bud and fight off the bug. So your parents are as safe as they can be. There's nothing more you can do.'

The wifie looks a bit relaxed about that. Fair to say she's not doing all the worrying here, though. He's just as bad as her. At least as bad. Twisting that armchair fabric into knots, isn't he?

'But there is something you can do to help me.' Shepherd waits for them to look over at him, finishing his tea like he's Miss Marple. 'I appreciate how delicate this matter is, but we gather you were involved in some sexual relationships with Isobel—'

'Woah, woah. We've done nothing with nobody called Isobel.'

'The woman with the mask?' Shepherd looks around the room. 'It turns out she'd been in this very room for a cosy bunk up.'

'Wait.' Ryan stops his twisting and puts his paw to his mouth. 'Katrin is Isobel?'

'Katrin?'

'Katrin Ninetails. Her name on Schoolbook. That's Isobel?'

'Dr Isobel Geddes. Yes.'

'The MSP?'

Shepherd sits there, sipping tea, like this is all cool. 'Right.'

'Christ.' Ryan stares over at his wife, but they're both as shocked as each other.

'You didn't know?'

'No.' Dawn is frowning. 'I mean, she had her mask on all the time. It was quite a turn on, actually. Couldn't get her to take it off, she wouldn't, and... She was in control.' She shakes her head. 'That was really *her*?'

'She was murdered on Friday night.'

'Christ.'

'Hence us asking you about it all. Did you see her?'

Another long, hard look. People in relationships like that, even when they get off on pegging in a builder from Lasswade, they've got this hidden code, this secret language.

'Okay.' Ryan sits back, hands splayed on his lap. 'Okay, we told you we were there. What else is there to say?'

'Did you have sex with her?'

'Tried to. But Isobel... She was popular. If that was really her. I mean, she controls people, right? Suggests stuff and, all of a sudden, everyone is into it.'

'Who was she with, do you know?'

'A man in a mask, I think. Tall, skinny as hell.'

Oh aye.

I shuffle forward on my seat and point at my cheek. 'You recognise him?'

'He had a mask on too.'

'Any identifiable features?'

Ryan frowns. 'Not that I can think of.'

'Ry!' Dawn is scowling at him. 'When you were going down on him, his mask slipped and there was this birthmark thing.' Lassie points to her right cheek.

Have to say, as good as it is peering inside these people's lives, it's a bit filthy isn't it? Might need a shower like Shepherd had back at the nick. But I doubt that'll clean anything up. 'You know him?'

She frowned. 'No.' Then the frown deepened. 'Oh, the birthmark!' She tugged at her husband's sleeve. 'I know who the skinny guy is, Ry! Remember I told you about the birthmark that guy had that you were going down on? I bet that was Peter Tomlinson.'

Isobel's ex.

I could give her the whole thing about "why didn't you tell us earlier?" but I can't be arsed. 'What else was going on here?'

'Well, if that *was* Isobel Geddes, she was ordering me around. The attention was flattering. She kept making us change positions. Thing is, Isobel was into being strangled.'

'Wait, I thought she was the top here?'

'You know the lingo, aye?'

'I do. But that would make Isobel a masochist. I know there's debate about who's ultimately in control in sado-masochistic relationships, but it doesn't add up to me.'

'Well, aye, Isobel's complex. She's very much into pain. Christ, I've never met anyone with even half her pain tolerance, but since lockdown started, she's changed. All the Covid stuff, it's made her get into edge play. And I'm not talking just a wee choke, but really close to death, going blue, medically flatlining, that kind of stuff. Extreme.'

And all while her hubbie dearest is noshing off Isobel's ex. Man alive, these people. 'Who was choking her?'

'Wayne loved to do it. He's a real sadist.' Dawn showed her left arm, where a big gouge was taken out. 'He did this to me.'

'Wayne?'

'Wayne Leonard.'

Figures, the ringleader. He was right up to his— Well.

15

Cullen took another look at Elvis, standing there scratching his balls with one hand, while his other tapped away on his phone with his over-developed thumb. Buxton sat in the passenger seat playing with his dentures.

What a team. Christ.

Cullen looked round at Methven. 'I'd much rather have Hunter here, sir.'

'Why?'

'Well, in case this guy runs. Craig is the—'

'We need to strike now, Scott.' Methven smoothed down his wiry eyebrows. 'Besides, I'm faster than Craig on foot.' Methven was a few inches taller than Cullen, and he was always banging on about his triathlons, but he was still pretty much skin and bone.

'But in a fight, sir? Much rather have Craig. Sorry.'

Methven smiled. 'We shall leave DC Gordon in the car. He finished top of his class in Advanced Driving.'

'No way.'

'I suggest you check up on your team's service record on a more-frequent basis, Inspector. As luck would have it, DC Gordon is a bit of a hot rod.'

All Cullen could do was raise his eyebrows. All he ever got

Elvis to do was donkey work. Running CCTV, phone records, anything technical. As much as he had an aptitude for it, he would make a dog's dinner of anything else.

'And besides, we're just here to ask him a few questions about a historic property transaction, that's all.' Methven walked over to Elvis and kept his distance as he gave the orders, slow and steady, answered with a series of nods.

It was way more than that, and Methven knew it. A connection that hadn't been owned up to. Never a good thing.

Cullen tried phoning Shepherd, but his call was bounced. Same with Bain. Bloody nightmare. And that was without thinking of the juice that Bain could be spilling to a potential mole.

No, Cullen had nothing to hide here. Of anyone, he was the cleanest. Well, he had some secrets, but didn't everyone?

He waved at the uniforms over the road and got a thumbs up. Their car drove off in a belch of thick diesel, heading round the back. Looked like fields, still, though the housing estates were beginning to encroach on it, just like down in Gorebridge. Not that there was much work going on just now.

Methven walked back over, all casual, hands in his pockets. 'Let's do this.' He led Cullen up to the door and tried the bell.

One of those fancy new ones, with that ascending chime. Probably meant they were being recorded, and on video too, with their presence being notified across the internet.

Leonard could be anywhere, and he'd know the police were onto him.

Either way, inside the house or not, Leonard wasn't answering the door.

Methven let out an almighty sigh. 'Well, that's just sodding marvellous.'

'Stay here.' Cullen took the perimeter anti-clockwise, his feet crunching over pristine pebbles. The side gate was a bit stiff, but he got it open with a grinding tear. The back garden was all boxed-in beds and raised decking, with a section housing a hot tub. The tub was warm, but cool enough that it was more like nobody had been in there in hours.

Quite the place, though not in the same ballpark as Wedale House.

Cullen made his way across the pebbled path, clocking the squad SUV trundling across the field at the back. Three downstairs windows, but there was no sign of anyone inside, even through the warping and distortion of the uPVC glass.

He checked the kitchen window, but it was show-home pristine now, no cups or plates or anything. Leonard had tidied up.

And he didn't seem to be home.

Cullen set off around the side of the house.

Methven had his head pressed against the door, eyes screwed up, mask raised over his eyebrows. 'I think there's someone inside.'

'Sure?'

'I can hear someone shouting.'

'Could be a cat.'

'Could be.' Methven snorted. 'But I don't want to take the chance.'

'Wise move.' Cullen stuck his head to the door and, sure enough, it did sound like someone shouting. Muffled and distant. But it also could've been a cat screaming to get fed. Whether the little sod was hungry was another matter.

Methven nodded at the door. 'On you go.'

No matter how high Cullen climbed through the ranks, he seemed destined to always have to smash through entrances. The positive side of Buxton's unfortunate recent incident was that Cullen was a bit more cautious now. Small things, such as trying the handle before launching himself shoulder-first.

And it opened wide.

And those were definitely a woman's muffled screams, not a cat's.

Methven barged in first, following the sounds up the staircase.

Cullen waved back at the car, until he got Buxton's attention and a thumbs up, then he piled up the stairs after Methven, their footsteps thumping hard on the bare wood.

Methven took the first door on the right, leaving Cullen with a choice between straight ahead and left.

The screams came from the left and were quicker and more desperate now.

A bedroom, beige paint on the walls, the furniture all dark wood. A woman lay on the bed, tied up, eyes wide with fear rather than arousal. Though the circles these people moved in, terror got confused with erotic.

Cullen made sure his mask was tightened, then raised his hands. 'I'm going to let you go, okay?'

The woman stared at him like he was going to kill her. Hair darkened with sweat, and plastered to her forehead. Green eyes, getting wider and wider.

'Just stay still.' Cullen reached over to the bonds around her wrists, a pair of silk ties, and started to undo them.

Cullen pulled the gag out of her mouth, and got a blast of some language he didn't recognise. Polish, maybe?

She gnashed at him with her teeth, but she was too far away, and something held her up, a rope hanging from the ceiling that he hadn't seen before.

Cullen waved his warrant card at her. 'Police.' He pointed at his chest. 'I am Scott.'

'Scotland?'

'No, Scott Cullen. I'm a police officer. Here to help you.'

She stared hard at him. However she'd got into this situation, the poor woman had no trust left whatsoever.

'Who did this to—?'

'Wayne!' Her voice was a hoarse scream. 'Wayne!' Then more guttural cursing.

But she let Cullen at her wrists. He tugged at the ties and freed her right wrist, and she worked her left free.

Something crashed outside the room.

Another thump, like something hitting a doorframe.

'Purple sodding buggery!' Methven, out of breath. 'Stop or I'll—'

Another thump.

Cullen raced out of the room.

Methven hit the banister, then flipped over and fell. He hit the stairs hard, then disappeared.

Cullen stood at the top, staring down the steps. Methven slid down the wooden stairs, not even screaming. Just deathly still. No sounds.

Something thudded off Cullen's head from behind.

16

'Luke, my man, can you explain something to me?' I'm driving along the road, the main one towards Pathhead, but it's only what passes for a main road round here. This bend, for instance, fully ninety degrees left, then at least the same again back the other way. Why? Why not sort it out?

And as ever, I have to tap the brake a bit too often on account of the bumhead in front of us. I mean...

Need to calm down here. Blood pressure and all that.

Shepherd's in the passenger seat. Honestly, when did being a cop become just fannying about on your moby all day? This boy's constantly on it, and not even talking to people. Texts. Maybe he's reporting to the mothership about what Cullen's team are up to. Here's hoping, eh? 'What?' He still doesn't look up.

'Mobile phones. You seem to be a bit of a connoisseur of the form.'

'Do I?' Still not looking up.

'Aye, anyway. When they came in, it was all about being able to contact people, right?'

'Still is, Brian.'

'I mean by phoning them. When I started on the force,

nobody had them. Maybe some City wideboys in London, right, or high-end drug dealers in Wester Hailes and Leith. But not coppers. Our radios were shite too, and anyone could hack in to them and hear what we were saying.'

He's sighing at us. 'Is there a point to this?'

I pull into yet another right turn, but at least we're in Path-head again, heading towards the new houses that weren't here the last time I was in this infernal town. Feels like five minutes ago, but it was probably ten years. 'Case in point. You're trying to get hold of Su— Cullen, or Cry— DCI Methven, to get approval for this dunt on the Leonard boy's home. And neither of them can bother themselves to answer.'

'Neither of them will be playing *Angry Birds*, though.'

'*Farmville*, maybe.'

'Brian, I've already got authority to do this.'

'Do you?'

'You've been a sergeant, you know the rules.'

'Aye, but I know the feeling of a size nine being lodged right up my bumhole.'

He actually laughs. Christ, maybe he wasn't made on a table somewhere. 'Relax, Brian, Cullen is only a nine in American sizes.'

'Aye?'

'No, he's an eleven if I remember right.' Shepherd waves his phone to the right. 'In there.'

I follow his lead and ease the motor round the bend. It's not quite like driving the Duchess this thing, but it's not that bad. Not that bad at all. A weirdo cul-de-sac, one of those ones where the houses are all looking away from each other, but with snidey wee viewpoints so they can keep tabs on each other, where you can see what everyone's up to. Makes you wonder why they bother. Must make the local Maureen's life a living hell, not being able to just twitch her curtains to keep an eye on what's going on outside. Having to peer round the bend? Drive her right round the bend.

Anyway, I get out onto the street and, lo and behold, there's a bottle-green Golf parked out front, just like Cullen's.

And Christ, is that Buxton? And Elvis? He's still not

speaking to us after that shite in America, so he just makes eye contact with us then looks away. I bore the brunt of all that, and he got off with it.

That's gratitude, eh?

Buxton though, he's keen as mustard, isn't he? That, or he's cowardly custard and soiling himself about that new sergeant turning up, even if Shepherd is just a temporary addition to the happy band. Buxton's marching over and I'm struggling not to picture that python of his swinging in his trousers.

Time I show everyone who's the best here, so I jog over to Buxton and meet the lad halfway. 'What are you doing here?'

'Waiting.' Buxton points to a house. 'Scott and Crystal are inside.'

'Seeing Wayne Leonard?'

'Yeah.'

'Why?'

'To see if he needs his double glazing redone. Why do you think?'

Shepherd's next to us, sticking his phone to his ear and using it like a normal human being for once. 'You got back up?'

'Me and Paul, plus a pair of uniforms in the field behind.'

'Stay with them.' Shepherd takes his phone away from his lug. Eyes narrowed, lips pressed tight together. 'Okay, Si, call the uniform and get an update.' He pats my arm as he brushes past. 'Come on, Brian.'

I follow the boy across the tarmac then up the fancy paving slabs to the house, all the while feeling that excitement surging in my belly. Probably walking into a fight here, or at least an opportunity to arrest someone.

Because this Leonard boy has been telling porkies.

'Try the door. I'll do a perimeter sweep.' Shepherd takes off down the side and the gate squeaks as he opens it.

A sweep. Christ, he thinks he's in the FBI.

I chap on the door, but it slides open inwards. Inviting me in.

Ah, Christ. A moral dilemma. Great. I hate them. Much rather do nothing. But that's a decision, isn't it?

No sign of Shepherd, so bugger it, I head inside. 'Hello?'

Place is empty. Tidy. Actually, it's almost too tidy, if you catch my drift. Boy must be a neat freak. And not like he's tidying up after kids all day, but like he's not put anything personal into his living space.

Serial killer alarm bells are ringing in my head.

Sounds like the party's going on up the stairs, though. Thumping and bumping. Maybe Cullen needs a hand from us, so I head towards the staircase.

FUCKIN' SHITE.

Methven is lying at the bottom. Eyes open wide, not quite staring at us. Not even breathing, by the looks of it.

Someone's definitely up there. Floorboards creaking. Trouble with these modern places, isn't it?

I try Shepherd's number but the arsehole bounces us. Christ, my hands are actually shaking here.

This is getting way too real for my liking.

Bugger it, I'll show Shepherd what's what here, show him how to do it.

I hammer out a text to Elvis, *GET IN HERE. CALL AMBU-LANCE*, and step over Methven's body, then climb the stairs.

Three doors up there, but the action's happening on the right. Christ on a bike.

Leonard is in there, and it looks like he's tying up someone. And with some bondage gear. Ball gag in the mouth, chains, the whole nine yards.

It's Cullen. Christ. He's barely conscious, but sort of looking in my direction. He grunts something.

Making Leonard look at us.

Well, there goes the element of surprise, doesn't it?

I snap out my baton but, Christ, the boy's *fast*. He drops his sex toys and lurches across the room towards us. I try and parry his blow, but he pushes my forearm into my teeth, and wraps a hand around my wrist. My baton clatters to the floor and rolls away.

I stumble back into the hall and grab the banister. Get a kick in the side, and I go down, but this side of it.

Leonard just stands there, maybe realising that he's

attacked three cops now. But he kicks my side and scarpers off down the stairs, the floor thumping as he jumps over Methven.

Cullen is lying there too. He looks out of it, might've suffered a brain injury. I can stay with him and save him, or I can try and catch that arsehole.

It's not much of a choice, is it?

17

'—Hear me?' Someone clicked their fingers in front of his face.

Cullen lay there, blinking hard. The light was too loud. No, too bright. Aye, that. 'Wuh?' Words were beyond him, even grunts were a struggle.

'Scott, can you hear me?'

It hit him. Methven. Falling down the stairs. Dying? 'Where's Methven?'

Shepherd's face loomed over him, frowning hard. 'You okay, Scott?'

'Where's Methven?'

Shepherd looked over to the side. 'In an ambulance, on his way to the Royal.'

Cullen felt something snap inside his head.

'Hard to say.'

Someone gripped his eyelids and a bright light shone into his skull. Then into the other eye. 'Doesn't seem concussed. He's lucky.'

Cullen was sitting on a bed. Same duvet cover as another one he remembered. 'The woman?'

'She's fine, Scott. Her name is Marta. Paula Zabinski's talking to her.'

'Where's Leonard?'

Shepherd scowled at him. 'We don't know.'

Cullen felt around the back of his skull at the tender lump forming. If he wasn't concussed, then he got off lightly. 'What happened?'

'I don't know. It's going to take a lot of unpacking.' Shepherd let out a deep sigh. 'All I know is, Bain came running out and—'

Bain.

Cullen saw his face, saw him standing in the hall. Then sitting down, leaning back against the banister like he'd been attacked too. He could've come to help Cullen, but he'd left. 'Where is he?'

'Drove off in a pool car.' Shepherd put his phone to his ear. 'Control, can you give me an update on the location of DS Bain's pool car?' He rolled his eyes. 'You said it was going to take a while five minutes ago.' He shook his head. 'No, an hour isn't a while, it's *ages*.'

Cullen tried standing and it felt like everything swum around, like he was underwater. If this wasn't concussion, he'd hate to feel that. He blinked hard a few times, rubbed at his aching left ear, and something seemed to clear in amongst it all.

Bain hadn't left him there out of mischief, he'd left him because he could still catch Leonard.

Maybe.

Best case.

Then again, it was Bain. Who knew?

Cullen grabbed the banister and took grandad's steps down the stairs.

The street was the same as he remembered, but just way too bright. The sunlight attacked his eyes, stinging with a dull ache.

Elvis was leaning against a pool car, holding a laptop in one hand, typing with the other. He frowned at Cullen's approach. 'Scott? You okay?'

'Not really. What happened?'

'Some boy came battering out, then got into his motor and drove off. Then Bain did the exact same.'

Cullen's turn to sigh now. Felt back in the game now, at

least, something to distract him from the pain. 'Paul, you should've gone after him.'

'But what if there—'

'There was a squad car in the field behind.'

'Right. Sorry.' Cheeky bugger was still focusing on his laptop. 'Got a lock on Bain's mobile location, if you want it?'

18

Thinks he's smarter than me, doesn't he? Well he can get to fu— France. I know these roads like the back of Little Brian, and I've hammered the Duchess around them a ton of times. Know where he's going before he's even at the bend before the one before he's going to turn.

Busy road, mind, busier than it's ever been. Bus hurtles this way, then a tractor covered in straw bales stops us overtaking and getting one ahead of him.

His brake lights glow up ahead, partly blocked by the Corsa in front, and he winds round the bend. Nothing coming for a bit.

Here we go, heavy foot and I hoor it around the bend on the wrong side of the road, getting the finger off the old dear in the Corsa as I blast past. Sorry, love, police business and all that jazz.

Obviously Leonard is taking the back road instead of going into Gorebridge, avoiding any roadblocks. Like I've had time to call anyone and get them to set up a roadblock or any of that nonsense.

But this is how I like it, hammering along the road now, just me and him. Past the new houses, looking across the wide plain to the Pentlands in the distance.

He's got a lead on me, as I don't know this exact stretch of road as intimately as the one back there, and I'm not driving the Duchess. This used to be a backroad, but now it's full of cars, and CHRIST some prick's pulled in, between me and Leonard.

Fuck sake!

Why is it arseholes always do that at the worst possible time?

I pull out to round him, but there's a bus coming the other way so I have to brake and pull back in. Christ!

But then he's staying on this road, and I start to recognise bits. Weaving around the more-familiar bends, the muscle memory's coming back.

Up ahead, Leonard's not slowing much at the thirty sign. Driving like a dickhead's not on the charge sheet these days, sadly. He shoots left into the belly of Gorebridge, still hammering it way faster than he should through the outskirts.

Wilson Road it's called, a winding drive through ex-council houses.

But by the third turning, there's no sign of Leonard.

Shite!

Oh no. There he is, down at the junction, indicating right.

By the time I've got over, he's at the next one, indicating left. Bareyknowe Lane sounds like it should be cute walls and hedges, but it's a straight run down past the new school and, of course, the kids aren't in, so it's dead and Leonard's hammering down.

I'm following as fast as this piece of shite will let me, battering over the speed bumps, knocking me up and down like a bastard.

And there's no trace of him at the end. The main road. Shite!

Can see better to the left, and it looks all calm. Serene. Not exactly the wake of a daftie running from the law doing sixty in a thirty.

Right, though, is bedlam. A couple of cars pulled onto the pavement, probably to let that weapon past.

So I swing round and another heavy boot. This thing's actually pretty fast. There's a wee sweet spot between fifteen and thirty on this bad boy where it jerks forward like a cougar. Oh, I'm growing to like it.

And, aye, there's Leonard up ahead, stopped at the lights. Thinks he's in the clear, thinks he's lost us.

But I've got him.

I should get out, run after him, but with these bloody knees, he'll have shot off before I've got my right foot down on the road.

I could try and ram him from behind, but it's pretty busy. That's the A7 up ahead, lorries and tractors and God knows what.

So I wait and, bingo, he's turning left.

I can take it a bit slower, ease off a few car lengths behind him, keep an eye on him naturally, make him think he's won, that this daft cop has fallen for it and is headed for Galashiels.

I drive on, past the new houses, then past the old farm buildings at the edge of town and out into open countryside on the main road north.

But no sign of Leonard.

Shite. There's a turning to the left, down towards Gore Glen, but he's not that daft.

So I head up to the roundabout, just in time to see him swinging round. Don't think he's clocked us as I follow the same manoeuvre, but I keep an eye on him.

Bingo, he's heading right down the narrow road to Gore Glen. Daft sod.

So I batter round the circle, as they'd say in bonnie Dundee, and swing back, then follow him down the country lane.

And the road is seriously awful, more potholes than tarmac. Rocking backwards and forwards, must be obvious that he's being followed from all the clanking and grinding this thing's doing.

But the sneaky sod is easing into the car park. Buggery, it's quiet now. No cop cars about.

So I take it really slowly, not least because that big bastard who maintains the cars won't be happy with us again, but also to figure out what Leonard's up to here.

And if I'm heading into a firefight here, I need to know.

I stop and take in the scene again. Start from first principles. Three cars, plus mine, plus Leonard's. A bridge leading to some fancy estate, or just a farm. God knows. A green gate blocks the way for cars, but an old retired couple are walking a clapped-out lab around it, heading away. And the dog hunkers down to do a big jobbie, oblivious to his owners. Other cars are empty.

Okay.

Leonard's talking to someone on his phone.

If there's a firefight, then it's not here yet.

I've got time.

I can do this.

So I nudge this beast of a car into neutral and let the hand-brake go, then let the hill do the work, slowly then faster, then I tap the brake behind him. I've blocked him in.

Now for the hard part. I get out and walk fast over the ground, reaching for his door handle.

He looks out as I'm about to touch it. And he shites it, eyes wide. The ignition growls, and he crunches back into my motor.

But I've got the door open and I grab his arm, down at the wrist, digging the thumb into the bone just like my old buddy in Dundee used to. Never fails, despite the fact this bugger's just beaten up at least three cops. Belt's off, so he tumbles out onto the mud.

'You're under arrest.'

'What for?'

'The assault of two police officers. I'm sure there's others.' Shite, I've not got my mask on and this boy's got Covid. Shite, shite, shite.

Ach well. Small price to pay.

I tighten my grip on. 'Come on, son, you'd better have a good lawyer.'

'The best.' His head's bowed as I frogmarch him over to my motor.

I'll call Control later to get someone to pick up his motor. Someone who can't drive, who might bump it off a lamppost. Nice piece, though, might drive it myself.

He lurches to the side, but I tighten my grip to let him know who's in charge here.

And shite, he goes down like a sack of spuds, sliding in that lab's jobbie. Fresh and reeking. And he pulls us down with him, and my hand lands in fresh dog keech, splatting up over my watch and up my wrist. Up my fuckin' sleeve.

Fuck sake!

I punch the cunt in the balls. Hard. No fuckin' mercy!

He screams and I'm standing over him and the old me would be booting him hard in the plums and just keep on kicking. Harder and harder and harder!

'Please!'

'Please?' I tower over him. '*Please*?! I've got dog *shite* up my arm! And you're a killer! You don't get to say please!'

'I can make it worth your while.'

That stops us.

'Let me go and I'll pay you. Whatever it takes. Just, please.'

Sneaky prick thinks he can get away with this, doesn't he? See these pricks with money, it's always the same with them, isn't it?

I sniff. 'How much we talking here?'

19

Ohe thing Cullen had definitely forgotten over the years was Shepherd's driving ability. While Cullen was in front, Shepherd was tearing along behind him, impatient to get ahead.

Cullen picked up his radio and put it to his head as he steered around the bend. 'Luke, you can overtake if you want.'

'Sure, I know that.' Cullen caught his broad grin in the rear-view. 'But I've got a trick up my sleeve.'

Shepherd hauled his pool Saab right, crossing almost in front of a tractor, and winding off up into Gorebridge.

'Luke?'

But he was gone.

Cullen picked up his mobile and checked he was still on with Elvis. 'You there?'

'Aye, sir!' A military shout, but laden with cheek and sarcasm.

'You got an update on Bain's location?'

'Aye, sir!'

'You want to tell me it?'

'Aye, sir!'

'Elvis, what the—'

'Take your next left, Scott.'

Cullen almost missed it. A narrow country lane, signposted for Gore Glen Country Park. The same one as that morning.

Where the body was, where it had lain at rest since Friday.

Why was Bain heading here?

Why was Leonard heading *back* there?

Cullen powered on, sliding downhill, then weaving under the old railway bridge, just like he did that morning, and still had no idea if the trains used it. He rocked over the potholes as he rounded the final bend.

Bain's car sat in the car park.

Cullen hammered the brakes and jumped out with the engine still running. He raced across the mud, but stopped at the back of the car.

Someone was groaning.

He snapped out his baton and eased forward, taking it one slow step at a time.

The groaning got louder.

Bain was kneeling by the open door, his face screwed up tight. He opened his eyes and looked at Cullen. 'Scott?' He winced again. 'Prick battered us in the goolies.'

'Leonard?'

'Aye. Shiiiiite.' He splashed vomit into the door pocket. 'Christ on a bike.'

Cullen held out a hand. 'Come on, let's get you upright.'

Bain grabbed it and let himself be helped up. A waft of dog mess followed him.

Bain sat on the passenger seat, fiddling with his groin. 'I lost him.'

Cullen checked his hand, but the gloves still looked box fresh. 'What happened?'

'What do you think happened? Chased him, caught him, prick tried to bribe us, I called in back-up, and he caught us right in the swingers.'

Cullen didn't know how much to believe of it. Bain had a tendency for being extremely untrustworthy, not to mention a reputation for it. Maybe he took that bribe, maybe there was money in his account, or even his wallet. 'Why didn't you stay with him?'

'Because the bastard nailed us in the goolies!'

Gravel crunched behind.

Cullen swung round.

A white work van sat there, engine running. Big Rob was behind the wheel, eyes wide, mouth hanging open. He pulled the van back, arcing round in a three-point turn. As he shot off back to Gorebridge, a pool car burst into the car park and boxed him in.

Hunter was behind the wheel.

Cullen's phone blasted out. He checked the display. Elvis had left the building, or at least the call.

Shepherd calling...

'Cullen.'

'Scott, is your radio off or something?'

'Sorry, I've recovered Bain.'

'Get out of the bloody way!' Horns blared in the background. 'Scott, I'm not ordering you, but get your car back on the road, I've got sights on Leonard!'

'Right.' Cullen jabbed a finger at Bain. 'Stay here!'

'Aye, like I'm going anywhere. Balls are in my ribcage.'

Cullen raced over to his Golf and waved at Hunter to stay with them. He got in, and the engine was still running, so he slid back, then arced round and darted the way he'd come, climbing the hill under the old bridge.

Then out into the open, ploughing down the country lane towards the A7. He could see in both directions for miles, but Gorebridge blocked the view ahead.

He spotted a dark-grey Saab on the roundabout to the left, looking like it was trailing a BMW.

'Luke, are you at the rou—'

'Yes!'

Cullen was at the junction. Just a few seconds and Leonard would shoot past. He pushed his Golf onto the road and clipped Leonard's BMW.

Cullen's airbag puffed out and almost smothered him.

Grinding and tearing, then a loud thud, followed by squeals.

Cullen batted the airbag away and tried to look along the road.

Leonard's car was at right angles to the roundabout, the front mounting the kerb. The driver door opened and Leonard flopped onto the pavement. His face was a bloody mess, covered in wild slashes like someone had attacked him with a machete.

Cullen put his foot down on the tarmac, but couldn't find his baton. Must've left it back at the park.

A blur of energy raced over and pinned Leonard to the ground.

Shepherd, uncut and unscratched, shaking his head at Cullen. 'And you say I'm a dangerous driver?'

20

I can't stand up. These plums of mine, well, if feels like they're no longer attached. That prick hit us so hard. That drive back from the arse end of Midlothian was painful, I tell you. Aside from being covered in dog shite, I should really be at the doctor's, but I've got to watch to see how this plays out, don't I?

And they're in the worst room in St Leonard's, too. Cullen and Shepherd are interviewing Leonard. Ha, the stupid prick's hardly a saint and, what's worse, he refused to bring a lawyer in. I mean, good way to implicate yourself, isn't it? Good way to bugger everything up.

'I wasn't even home at the time in question.'

No sooner have I sat down, but the door opens and wee Eva pops her head through. Doesn't look like it's me she wants to see, mind.

'How's it going, Eva?'

'How do you think? That arsehole Cullen has got me doing the ANPR shite instead of Elvis.'

'Well, the lad's done more than his share of it.'

'Aye, but—'

'Anyway, you find anything?'

She passes over the usual ANPR output. Long list of hits

from Wayne Leonard's beemer. 'Have a look at this.' She passes another one.

I take one look and Leonard is *scubbed*.

Timestamped screen grab of him sitting in a car, while that Polish lassie gets in. Marta? Maria? Either way, I don't know if she's a hooker or what, but his balls are nailed to the wall here.

Saturday morning, too.

After he'd murdered Isobel. Bad, bad boy.

'Cheers, Eva.'

Looks like she wants to take it back off us, but she's also smart enough to let it slide. 'I've got more to check, but that seems good.'

'I'll make sure Cullen hears all about it.'

'Thanks.' And the door slides shut behind her.

Sod this for a game of soldiers. I follow her out, catch a glimpse of her striding away down the corridor.

That big-cocked fanny Buxton slides past her. Christ, imagine him shagging her? He clocks us. 'Seen Scott, mate?'

'He's busy. Why do you need him?'

'Why do you think?' Buxton stops just out of swinging distance. 'Me and Elvis are speaking to Big Rob, but he ain't playing ball.'

'And you need Scott Cullen to help out?'

'He's the DI, yeah.'

I crack my knuckles. Get a wee twinge in the balls, but it's nothing. I've got this, and got it good. 'Show me the way.'

Buxton follows Eva down the corridor. 'He's in four.'

I open the door and pop my head in. Elvis is sitting there with that big bastard.

Big Rob. What a guy. More muscle than sense, but he's got way too much bulk, and bugger all smarts.

Not that Elvis is paying us any attention. Gives us one wee look, then away. He got hosed when we came back from America. Feel bad for the boy, a bit, but it's his fault as much as mine.

So I sit in the seat Buxton's just vacated. 'Right, mate.'

Big Rob just narrows his eyes at us.

'Got a wee puzzle, son. Why your motor just so happened to

be pulling up at the same place and time as a lead suspect in a murder investigation. Care to help us with that?'

He shrugs.

'Like that, is it?'

'Yeah.'

'Son, you're up to your conkers in your own shite here. Not only did we have to drag you out of a cage, covered in literally your own excrement...' I get a whiff of dog shite just then, 'you're meeting up with Wayne Leonard at the park.'

'He's a mate.'

'A very good one, too.' I lean over the desk and try to get that right hissing voice. 'Son, why don't you just say what's in your heart? The truth, nothing but it. How about that?'

He looks at Elvis next to me, then Buxton by the door, then back at us. 'Fine. He asked me to a meeting at the park, but he didn't show.'

'He phoned you?'

'No, it was a prior arrangement.'

'What for?'

Big Rob grins. 'Asked me to chop down a tree in his garden.'

'Bollocks. I've been in that garden, not so much as a blade of grass, let alone a tree.'

'It's a business thing.'

'Aye?'

'I don't have to say anything, do I?'

'Nope.' I put Eva's printout on the table, face down. 'But Mr Leonard is in a big heap of trouble. Way I see it, you were there to help him out. That's trouble with the cops, big time. Now, you're already a person of interest here, so I suggest you spill. Everything. Now.'

The boy doesn't need much time to think it through, likes. 'Fine.' He swallows down a sigh. 'We were meeting because... Look, from what I gather, Leonard had to sell Wedale House. Okay? That's how he met Isobel. Back in 2008. Ran out of money, couldn't pay the mortgage, had to get out otherwise he'd lose all of his money. Parental inheritance kind of deal. Trouble is, he'd buried something in the garden.'

Elvis leans forward, just like I did. Sorcerer's apprentice, alright. 'So, it's these pills we found, right?'

Pills? What pills?

Rob nods at the boy. 'Right.'

'Are they illegal?'

'Not sure.'

'That because you don't know? Or because their legality is yet to be determined?'

'Bit of both.'

'But you've no idea what they are?'

'No. None.'

'Did Mr Leonard tell you how he came to get them?'

'From what I gather, he'd asked Isobel to access them but she refused. When he found out about her and me, he got me to ask. I tried, but she said no. They're hidden under a rose bush she particularly likes.'

'But now she's dead?'

'Well...'

Elvis rests a page on the table, face up. 'Wayne got in there yesterday.'

Rob barely looks at it.

'Bastard, eh?' Elvis laughs. 'Knew you were downstairs and he let you rot?'

'Aye...'

'So why you, son? Surely your use expired when you couldn't get hold of the pills? He did it himself when he knew she was dead. So why you?'

'I know a guy.'

'You know a guy?'

'At my gym. Used to deal steroids and ... other stuff. He knows how to shift pills. I was to give him the drugs, and get the money back.'

Ya dancer.

I lean over to Elvis. 'Keep him talking. I'll see what his mate's got to say about all this shite.' I grab his shoulder on the way up, not to support myself, just to show there's no animosity here, and also that, well, that's how you do it, you clown.

I leave the pair of numpties to it, and I could whistle as I stroll along the corridor towards the room Cullen and Shepherd are in. But that would be unprofessional, and Brian Bain is nothing if not a pro.

I open the door and stand there, soaking it in.

The smell of fear in both interviewee and the interviewing cops.

Is he going to get done?

Are they going to make a mess of this?

Oooh, the suspense is killing me.

'How many times do I have to go over this? I wasn't there when you say I was, and you can't prove I was.'

I slip in like a ghost, except not like passing through stuff and all that ghosty lark, and lean against the back wall.

Let them all stew, cops and suspect.

Let them all wait.

I keep the timestamped printout to myself.

'Sure.' Shepherd's a cool cucumber, isn't he? Actually, I could do with something like that for my nadgers. 'Except for the fact that three serving officers stated your presence at the property, as does Marta Wislowska.'

That's her name. Marta.

Leonard's frowning at us, the only one of the three to pay any attention. 'Marta who?'

Shepherd laughs. 'You saying you don't know the name of the woman you had tied up in your bedroom?'

'If there was a woman there, then it's nothing to do with me.'

'Why are you still denying this?'

'Because I had nothing to do with any of it.'

'You didn't find Marta on a website called "Zbigniew Boniek" fan club? Hope I'm pronouncing that right.'

'Who's he?'

'Footballer. Played for Juve in the eighties.'

'More a rugby man.'

'Same here. Had to google the name. But that website is known to our vice squad. Good way to meet Polish prostitutes.'

'Take your word for it.'

'So you're saying you didn't arrange to meet Marta on that site?'

'No.'

As much as I say Cullen is a useless bastard, as often as he proves it, this time he must know the game's afoot, as he swings round to look at us, frowning, then gives us a wee nod.

Enter centre stage, Brian Bain. I pass that nod on to Wayne Leonard. Here goes. I shuffle over to the side of the table as fast as my ruptured scrotum will allow, and slide the page across the scored wood. 'You didn't collect her from the car park at the Ashworth's supermarket in Eskbank?'

Leonard doesn't even look at it. 'Did I hell.'

'Okay, but you did push DCI Colin Methven over the banister in your house, right? You seem to have broken his spine.'

'Wasn't me.'

Shepherd sits back, arms folded. Boy gives away too much, doesn't he? 'Must've been a wee bit of a shock to find out Isobel was dead, right?'

'Eh, right.'

'I mean, you'd known it was her for a while, eh? That mask she wore didn't fool you.'

'No.'

'So, when you learnt that she'd died, how long did it take for you to get down to Stow?'

'Excuse me?'

I reach into my pocket for the other bit of paper Eva gave me, the ANPR results. 'Took a wee drive this morning, didn't you? Obviously before you went to the big Ashworth's in Eskbank, you had a nice wee drive down to Stow.'

'I was going fell running up in the hills.'

'Right.' I rest the pages between Cullen and Shepherd on the desk. 'Weird how there's a security camera catching you parking on the main road, then walking up Church Wynd.'

That's shut him up. I like to call it the quiet before the storm. When they've realised they're scubbed, but they can't own up to it yet. It's *delicious*, quite frankly.

'You want to tell us why you were there, Mr Leonard?'

Last thing he wants to do. He's quiet and staying that way.

I tap the page, him walking like one of the seven dwarves hi-hoing his way to work. 'Why the spade?'

He's going a wee bitty red here. Oh, the poor wee lamb.

'Way I hear it from a little birdie, you were digging to get at some stuff buried in her garden.'

Leonard's scratching at the stubble on his chin. Bullshit artist. And here comes another masterpiece. 'I left something there when I moved out.'

'In 2008?'

'Yes, but the item was buried in 2005. It had tremendous sentimental value.'

'What was it?'

Boy goes quiet again. Not even chucking paint off a canvas, so much as painting a Rembrandt.

'It wasn't a load of sex pills, was it?'

Nailed. He's looking right at us, though. Can see it in his eyes — he knows he's scubbed, and he knows just how scubbed he is.

'Why bury them?'

'They were worthless.' Leonard sits back with a sigh. 'Paid a ton of money for them, but then they became illegal. All that legal highs stuff? People couldn't get prosecuted because the individual pills weren't illegal, but then they flipped it so everything was illegal unless otherwise stated. So I had to get rid of them. It was part of my later financial troubles.'

'So why dig them up? Why get Big Rob to fence them?'

'Because I've heard someone was selling them as anti-5G pills.'

Cullen's ears prick up now. 'These are hydroxychloroquine?'

'Nope, but people will buy any old shite if they think it'll help. So my Mexican sex pills are worth a packet now. Way more than back then.'

'So you broke in and took them?'

'Right. But they were mine. My property.'

'Did you kill her?'

Leonard frowns. 'It's not as simple as that.'

'Enlighten me.'

'I'd asked Isobel to get them back. Even offered to pay, but she wouldn't... She wouldn't... It's partly a control thing with her, so I begged. That didn't work.'

'And she didn't take the money?'

'No.'

'Okay, so let's cut the crap. Who killed her?'

'It was part of her fantasy. You see that cave, it's like an altar. She was lying on there while I was thrusting at her, like she was being sacrificed. All the while, Ryan Marshall was working away at her ex-husband. That was the biggest turn on for her, I think. Seeing him suffer like that, but the glimmer of hope... But I could see how angry the whole thing was making Dawn.'

'Dawn Marshall?'

Wayne nodded. 'Isobel started to love being choked while we go at it. It's the only way she can ... get there. Dawn was doing the honours, but she didn't stop. Didn't heed the safe-word. Just kept going.'

Jesus Christ. These people. I mean, consenting adults and that, but man alive.

21

'Sundance, you look like you're wearing someone else's shoes and just found that they've shat in them.'

Cullen couldn't bring himself to even look at Bain. 'Says the man who is still wearing dog shit.'

'Eh?' But Bain was checking over his wrists and sleeves. 'Ah, Christ's sake. I'll never be clear of this!'

Cullen couldn't enjoy Bain's misery for long. 'I thought it was Leonard who killed her. Just couldn't figure out why.'

'We all did, Scott.'

'Right.' Cullen looked down at his shoes, and it did feel like they were someone else's. 'Letting those two arseholes live out their weird murder fantasy? And just standing there while they killed her?' He couldn't taste or smell anything, just like when he had Covid-19. He took a deep breath, but only had a slight rattle in his chest. 'I mean...'

'You can thank me, you know?'

'Eh?'

'For solving the case. Again.'

'Come on, that was Eva and Paul's work. Not yours.'

'Aye, but I pieced it together. And I got that big galoot talking. Then I showed how to get in there and get Leonard talking.'

Cullen stared at him, and it felt like he was looking at an

alien life form that nobody had encountered before. Some completely different way of seeing things, of processing things. And yet he'd encountered this strange beast so many times before. Way too many times. 'You left a crime scene.'

'Going to hold that against us, are you?'

'There were two injured officers present. And a woman tied up in the bedroom.'

'Scott, this case would be wide open if I hadn't tailed the boy!'

'Stop shouting.'

'Okay, but you need to listen to me here. I'm *the man* on this case.'

Cullen couldn't help himself from laughing. 'You're the man?'

'Aye. The. Man.'

Another laugh, but one that caught in Cullen's lungs. 'Right.'

'What's that supposed to mean?'

Cullen stared deep into those insect eyes. 'Ever since I first worked with you, you've been an arrogant sod, always thinking you're the best. Everyone else is the worst. I'm sick of it, and I'm sick of you.'

Bain laughed. 'Well, it won't be long until I'm not your problem.'

'You're leaving?'

'Nope. You are.'

'Shut up.'

'Serious here. Big Luke Shepherd is investigating you.'

That chilled Cullen's marrow. 'What?'

'Boy's been asking all about you. I mean, someone's airing your dirty breeks in public on that Secret Rozzer podcast.'

Cullen winced. 'I know it's you.'

'Well, you've lost the plot, 'cos that is nothing to do with me.'

'You're lying.'

'Nope, but I have listened to it. Maybe even devotedly.' Bain licked his lips slowly. 'And you of all people should know not to accuse people of telling stories about you, especially when those stories are not good ones to be associated with.'

Cullen felt short of breath, like he was stuck in the depths of his illness.

'I mean, it's fictionalised, isn't it? Johnny Public won't know who it is, but anyone who knows Scott Cullen will recognise enough in it, and they will know you're dodgy.'

'I'm not.'

'Sundance, you fuckin' are. And Shepherd is here to take you down.'

'Are you seriously denying that it's you?'

'Of course I am.'

'If it's someone else, you've given them info, haven't you?'

'Get over yourself, Scott.'

'Who is it?'

'I don't *know* know, but I have a good idea.'

A lot of shit had been leading up to this point. Cullen wanted to lamp him, wanted to grab his wrist and twist his arm behind his back, even if it was covered in dog shit. He wanted to force Bain to the floor and get him to admit he was the Secret Rozzer.

But could Cullen ever believe him?

No, and someone like Bain took great care in embroidering and watermarking their stories so he'd know where they came from, who had been talking.

Cullen knew he couldn't win here. He pointed down the corridor. 'The rest of the team are having some drinks in the Incident Room. Head there if you think you deserve it.'

'What about you?'

'You'll see.'

22

W ho does that prick think he is?
You'll see?
You'll see?
You'll *see?*
You'll see?

I slam the fire door, but it just does its slow shutting thing. Christ's sake.

As much as I wish I was doing that podcast, it's not like I even can. Elvis has all that technical knowledge, worked all the magic. I was just the talent, the hero of the hour who people flocked to.

And it's not like Elvis is even speaking to me anymore, so I'm absolutely snookered. No, I'm scubbed.

The last few months, I've been pussyfooting around a bit too much. Wanting to nail Cullen, get him kicked off, but I made a right mess of that, especially when his Acting DI gig got made full-time, and the prick got me demoted.

Oh yes, Sundance needs to get taken down a peg or three.

So, here goes nothing.

I get out my moby and find the number. "Break in case of emergency".

Well, Past Me had a sense of humour that Current Me

doesn't have. Hopefully Future Me will look back on this pair and smile.

I hit dial and wait, then peek around the corner.

The Incident Room is looking pretty rammed already.

Can see Buxton and his love truncheon through the open doors, clutching a glass. Wee Eva Law comes out and gives us a wave.

I wave back.

'Carolyn Soutar's office, Elaine speaking.'

'Elaine, it's your favourite Edinburgh cop.'

'DC Bain.' She needs to practise hiding that groan.

'Is Her Ladyship around?'

'No, she's out of the office all afternoon. Apparently an officer was involved in a serious incident in Midlothian.'

'Aye, I was there. Wanted to share a few details about it.'

'Sure she'll appreciate it.'

'I need to speak to her tonight.'

She pauses. 'Okay. I'll get her to call you.'

'Cheers.' I end the call and actually feel a few stone lighter as I walk over to the Incident Room. Bliss.

Eva holds out her pack of ciggies for us. 'Want a smoke outside?'

'I'm fine.' And I should head inside and get a pint of turps, but I stay here with her. 'How you doing, Eva?'

'Bored.'

'Working for Cullen is so great, isn't it?'

'Damn right. He had me looking through CCTV all day.'

'I know. You gave me the stuff. You finding Leonard picking up that Polish lassie really helped us.'

'Right. Elvis is supposed to do that, isn't he?'

'But you solved the case, my girl. Well done.'

'Really?'

'Aye.'

Her eyebrows almost hit the ceiling. She looks really pleased.

The doors clatter open and that one with the Polish surname, Paula something, staggers out, already *battered*. She looks up at us. 'Brian?'

'Hey, Paula. How you doing?'

'Okay.' And there it is, the swaying of the shit-faced. She's clutching an empty bottle of white wine. Know what they say about white, eh? Just don't do it, kids. 'Christ, that Shepherd can ask questions, can't he?'

'Trying to get in your knickers?'

'I wish. Keeps asking about Scott bloody Cullen.'

'Oh aye?'

'Aye. Wish Chantal wasn't sick. Spoke to her today. Sounds like hell.'

'Doesn't it just.' Though I've no idea what she's talking about.

'Way I hear it, Chantal caught Covid psychically.'

Christ on a flaming Harley Davidson. '*Psychically*? What are you talking about.'

'Like, don't believe me if you want, but it's a thing. Google it.'

Is it shite a thing.

And Eva knows it too, judging by her big grin.

But Paula's a cracking gossip, so I don't want to call her on this bollocks. 'Lovely day, isn't it?'

'Is it?' Paula's face changes like the weather in this godforsaken city. 'My marriage is falling apart.'

Christ.

She's further gone than I expected. Or is a bigger lightweight. Her cheeks are all rosy, but her eyes are pure black. 'It's... He's cheating on me.'

'You've not been married long, have you?'

'Too long, Brian. Far too long.' She puts the wine bottle to her lips and almost misses it. Then slurps it down. This is a bad idea. Someone's going to have to get her home. She looks at Eva, then at me. 'Either of you ever banged a guy with a massive cock?'

'I'm not gay, Paula.'

'Eh?' She's scowling at me. 'Course you are.'

'No, I'm not.'

'Well.' Paula shrugs and takes another swig from the empty bottle. 'I can't stop thinking about this story Chantal told me. A few years ago, before Craig, she had an affair with a well-hung guy. And I can't stop thinking about it.' Then she stumbles off towards the bogs. Her wine bottle's in a plant pot, upside down.

Through in the Incident Room, I can see Hunter taking a pint of beer off Buxton, and it doesn't take Sherlock Holmes to put two and two together, does it? Or two inches and twelve.

Christ, imagine that?

'Eva, make sure you get some water into her, aye?'

She nods at us. 'Malky was asking about you.'

That stops us in my tracks. 'Was he, now?'

'Oh aye.'

I want to go and cause absolute havoc in there, but I look round at Eva. 'Got a few stories for your boyfriend if he's up for it.'

She nods, but doesn't make eye contact. 'He wants to record another podcast tomorrow. It's going *crazy*. The Secret Rozzer, eh? Magic.'

23

Of all the cops on pick-up duty, Cullen wouldn't have picked Elvis first. Like when he would play football at school break, Elvis would've been one of the last kids waiting. Not a sportsman by any stretch, but he did have other uses. Like his mad driving skills, shooting around whichever Midlothian backroad they were on. Cullen had lost track a few turnings ago.

'So, that Shepherd boy was asking me about you.'

As much as he didn't want to, Cullen looked over to get a read on Elvis, but he was laser-focused on his driving. 'What was he asking about?'

'Didn't speak to me directly, but he's been chatting to Eva, Paula, Craig, Si, you name it.' Elvis snorted. 'Right. Here we go.'

Cullen looked up and right he was, they were outside the Marshalls' home. 'Why didn't he ask you?'

'Eh...' Elvis sniffed. 'No idea.'

'Not because you're the Secret Rozzer?'

'Hardly.'

'Is it Bain?'

'Look, I know you asked me to dig into it, Scott, but I've been too busy. What I do know is it's not Bain.'

'This better not be a lie.'

'It's the truth, Scott. I've got all his podcasting gear. When

we, eh, had our wee falling out after America, I nabbed it all
back. He's totally clueless about the tech side. And the missus
was round theirs to show off the new baby. She said their
podcasting room is now a nursery.'

'A nursery.'

'Aye. Look, I did some digging into the feed. The server
where it's stored isn't owned by him, I know that much.
Someone in Edinburgh, but not him.'

Nothing conclusive.

Cullen clocked Shepherd's car in the rear-view. 'Okay, Paul,
I believe you for now. Stay put, and be prepared to shoot off if
they get wind of us, okay?'

'On it.' Elvis ran his fingers round the wheel, like he was
caressing something.

Cullen didn't want to think what, so he got out onto the
windy street. Some kids kicked a football over a back garden
fence, the ball arcing high up in the blue sky. Cullen used to do
that when he was young. Felt like forever ago.

'Scott.' Shepherd walked over, hands in pockets, all calm
and collected, and looked to the side. 'How do *you* think we
should play this?'

'Think we should get someone round the back.' McKeown
was with him, his shifty eyes narrowing.

Shepherd pointed towards the football flying through the
air. 'Go and see if you can get into their garden that way.'

'Sarge.' McKeown sloped off, hands in pockets.

Shepherd watched him go. 'Any idea how you turn his
brain on?'

'Wish I knew, Luke. Wish I knew.'

'You've not half got a bunch of dafties in your squad, Scott.'

'Swapping them for good cops takes a lot of time and work.
We're halfway there, at most. Besides, Malky's good for opera-
tions like this. That thick skull of his can take a lot of battering.'

'Aye, well, he's not good for driving, that's for sure.' Shepherd sniffed. 'So, you and me taking the front door? Like old
times?'

'Aye, let's.' Cullen held up a finger to Elvis, getting him

primed and ready. 'Shouldn't have let them go from the nick, should we?'

'Happens, doesn't it?' Shepherd stepped up the path and knocked on the door. 'Plus, they had a plausible story.'

'Just one that is absolute bollocks.'

'Not absolute, Scott. But omitting details like the fact they murdered Isobel Geddes.'

The door opened to a crack and an eye appeared, above a tattooed neck. Ryan Marshall. 'Aye?'

'Police.' Shepherd held out his warrant card. 'Need a word, sir.'

The door closed and opened up. 'What's this about?'

'Ryan Marshall, I'm arresting you for—'

The door slammed and Ryan disappeared into the house.

'Bollocks.' Shepherd shouldered it open, then stormed through.

Cullen followed, but Shepherd slipped into the lounge. 'Get after him!'

Cullen caught a glimpse of Shepherd guarding over Dawn Marshall and her kids, then he stormed through the kitchen. The back door was hanging open, so he pushed through and out into a garden.

A football cracked off his cheek, stinging like crazy. He looked around, but stars filled his vision.

Ryan was hanging over the wall.

Cullen sprinted over and grabbed his ankles, tugging Ryan's jeans down and showing a bit too much arse cheek. Then McKeown's head and forearm appeared and Ryan tumbled back onto Cullen.

As well as his stinging cheek, Cullen was now winded. He tried to push himself up to standing, but had to suck in a deep breath.

Ryan was weaving between the clotheslines, heading back to his kitchen door.

'Get after him!' Cullen tried to follow, tried to cajole McKeown into following. 'Now!'

McKeown was able to get to the kitchen, at least, but Cullen followed him into an empty room, just McKeown standing there scratching his neck.

Shepherd was through in the hall, cuffing Dawn.

Cullen searched the small kitchen, all white units and appliances. 'Where is he?'

McKeown opened a door to a garage.

Ryan stood by the far wall, holding a machete, covered in dried blood. 'Back off!'

Cullen stepped into the cold garage, palms raised. Boxes piled high on all sides. Bikes and prams. The street door was one of those that swung up, very hard to open from the inside. Cullen had him. 'There's nowhere to run, Ryan.'

'Get back!' He lashed out with the machete.

Cullen felt the air lash across his face. 'Give it to me, Ryan. Please.'

Ryan held the machete towards him. 'I can't.'

'Face up to what you've done, Ryan. You killed someone. You slashed their face and left them to rot. You're going to spend a lot of time inside for this. But I know you're not in control here, right? You didn't kill Isobel. That's not on you. Your ordeal is over.'

'I can't do this.' Ryan held the machete out at arms reach, then moved to plunge it towards his own heart.

A blur flashed past Cullen, and thudded Ryan into the wall. A clatter of metal on the floor, then Malky McKeown emerged holding the machete by the handle.

~

CULLEN HATED STARING into the eyes of a psychopath. But he didn't know who was worse, Dawn Marshall sitting in the interview room on his left, her husband in the room across the corridor, or Wayne Leonard being led away to the holding cells, head bowed.

None of them seemed to care what had happened to Isobel Geddes. Dying like that, to further some stupid moneymaking scheme with buried drugs, or just their sexual pleasure, whatever form that took.

Killing someone.

Cullen shut the door so he couldn't see Dawn any longer, leaving her with two of Shepherd's team.

Shepherd came out of Ryan's room, leaving McKeown behind him. 'Full confession, Scott. Malky's just dotting the I's and crossing the T's.'

Cullen let out a deep breath. 'You look like you could do with a drink.'

'I'm teetotal these days.'

'Pretty much the same myself.' Cullen laughed. 'But our teams have done well today. Let's make sure they have a good time.'

'Sure that's a good idea?'

Cullen grinned. 'The station's dead and Soutar's called in a favour to bring some in to the Incident Room.'

24

Cullen's team are standing in the Incident Room, hanging about, masks off, getting absolutely blunted. If the press got wind of this...

The boy manning the table looks familiar, ruddy-faced old bugger serving out beer and wine. 'What you having, Brian?'

As much as I don't recognise him, I can't for the life of me remember the round. Buggeration. 'Eh, six IPAs, and two glasses of white.'

'Large or small?'

'Large.'

Off he goes to the pumps. Actual beer. In a police station. Maybe I should give one of those lads at the *Argus* a tinkle, sure they'd love it. Or save it for Malky's podcast. And it's an okay IPA, too, I'll give him that, far from the best, but then it's hard to track down that IPA from the Florida panhandle, isn't it?

He passes two perfectly poured pints over. 'Old Inspector called us up, knew I'd have stock going off. These barrels are still fine.'

'You own a pub?'

'Aye, The Cheeky Judge.'

Got it.

The coppers' bar, just staggering distance from the back entrance to St Leonards. But it's not that. Maybe it's just that it stands to reason the boy's an ex-cop and, let's be honest, they all look the same, don't they?

Eva squeezes in next to us. 'Alright, Brian, Malky just texted us. You okay to come round tomorrow after your shift?'

Thing about her is she's not subtle. 'Aye, I'll have a look at those LPs. Why's he getting rid of them again?'

She frowns at us for way longer than she should, then it hits her. 'Oh. Aye. Right, well, we've just not got the space with him moving in to mine. It's so tight it's just tragic.'

'Aye, I'll probably take the lot off him, then. Only got the *Songs: Ohia* stuff on CD, so having it on vinyl would be fantastic.'

She rolls her eyes at us, playing along like a pro. 'You don't need to talk in code here. He's one of us.'

I frown at the barman. 'You know him?'

She looks back at us, smirking. 'Where do you think Malky's got half his material from?'

'Okay, so remind me what his name is again?'

'Willie McAllister. Used to work the beat down in Leith. Hates Cullen even more than you or I do.'

And it hits us. The bald dome, the smears of eyebrows, the snide look. Aye, I remember him now.

That case, way back when, he made an arse of something, didn't he? Some missing woman, who wasn't so much missing as dead.

Still, I focus on Eva. 'Still don't get why you hate Cullen so much.'

She shakes her head. 'He led me on is why. He's such a slag.'

'Isn't he just.'

Willie passes us four of the pints. 'Here you go, son.' He grins at Eva. 'You're not allowed to drink white wine after last time.'

'I didn't ask for white.' She scowls at us, then back at Willie. 'I asked this idiot for a Bacardi and Coke.'

'Can't get the staff, eh?' Willie slides over to the spirits. 'Malky doing okay?'

'Okay enough, Willie.' Eva stands there in the middle of the

Incident Room like it's a pub and she owns the place. 'You still trying to sell up?'

'On the QT, aye.' Willie rests her glass down with a huff that might've got some spit in her glass, but she either doesn't notice or doesn't care. 'Thinking I'll have to put it on the open market, when that's a thing again.' He's pouring the last pint incredibly carefully. 'Trouble is, anyone swooping in to buy a cop's bar, they'll turn it into something else, won't they?'

'Ruin the place for us.' Eva wrestles the four pints into formation, then powers across the floor to the huddle near where Cullen runs his morning briefings.

I take the fifth pint and sink a good few fingers. Braw. 'You really selling that place?'

He looks up from pouring the wine. Not using one of those metallic measuring things, either, just a lovely free pour like he's in some dive bar in the States. 'Trying to, aye. Got myself a house up in Applecross, but I need to sell this place before the buyers get too pissed off with me.'

'What's wrong with the pub?'

'Thought when I retired that sticking my life savings into it would give me all the good stuff from being a cop. You know, being around people all day. But it's empty most of the time, and when you're sober behind the bar, the people are all mostly wankers.'

'I hear you.'

He slides the two glasses of wine over. 'That everything?'

'Let's you and me have a chat about doing a deal.'

'You serious?'

'Might be. Got an inheritance coming, could do with something to coast me through retirement.'

But he's not listening now, his eyes are on the door. 'Robocop?'

Prick in a mask wanders in, doesn't he? Cullen, hands in pockets, smiling at us both. 'Hi, Willie. Pour another round for everyone, would you?'

I take my pint below halfway. 'I've got the motor.'

'You smell like you shouldn't be driving, Brian.' Cullen does that sigh of his. Makes him sound like a total dick. 'Just a Coke for me.'

'Not like you to not take a drink.'

'Driving too.' Cullen grabs the two wine glasses and takes them over to the whiteboard, where Elvis is drawing cartoons of everyone.

'Still a wanker, then?' Willie starts pouring a beer.

'And the other end of it.' I look outside and it's a glorious day. Bollocks to it, I'll get Apinya to pick us up. 'Throw in a shot with each pint, would you?'

Willie shoots us a wink. 'Coming right up.'

I take the first pair of pints off him and add in Eva's Bacardi. But I don't set off straight away. 'I'll come in one night this week so you and me can have a wee chat about me taking over your pub.'

'Any time.'

I head over to hand Eva her glass and rest my pint down on a table. Sod it. Not enough mayhem here, so I wander over to goad Hunter and Buxton. 'Boys.'

Hunter is sipping from his beer, slowly like it's lager. 'Brian.'

I take the seat between them. 'Braw day, isn't it?'

Hunter rests his beer on the table. 'You can't just sit there, acting like what Leonard did to Cullen and Methven is okay. Acting like running off like that is okay.'

He's got his bloody knickers in a right twist, hasn't he? 'Craig, I had to choose, didn't I? Sure you've been in that kind of situation. Over in Iraq, maybe?'

Oh, ya dancer. There's that wee pause, where he drifts off somewhere else. But he's back. 'Of course I have, but you left two colleagues. That's not cool. Shepherd reckons Methven might never walk again.'

'Right, but what am I going to do about that? I'm not a spinal surgeon, you fanny.'

He just looks at Buxton, like he's going to get backup from that boy.

'Time for a piss.' Buxton stands up and heads inside.

'Fetch the rest of the round, would you?'

'Sure.' And he buggers off.

But I fix my hardest stare on Hunter. 'Craig, the reason we caught Leonard is because of my actions. And I got battered in the nadgers for my troubles.'

'I'll punch you in the balls if you don't bugger off.' And it looks like he means it. Snide bastard.

But Buxton's turned up with the beers already.

'Christ, that piss was fast.' I smile at him. 'Suppose it's got a bit of a way to travel, so you have to start peeing five minutes before you need to, eh?'

Can tell he's not enjoying this. He sits down next to Hunter and hides behind his beer.

I finish mine, though. I run a hand across my lips but I can *still* smell the dog shit from earlier. Christ. 'Weird seeing you two sitting together like this. All pals.'

Hunter frowns at Buxton, then at me. 'What's that supposed to mean?'

'Well, you know about Chantal shagging Buxton, right?'

Hunter's gone red. 'What?'

'Heard it on the grapevine, Craig. Few years ago, but this boy's packing a monster cock. Doubt you can measure up to that! Imagine how disappointed Chantal must be to deal with your maggot after Buxton was banging her with that python!'

Ow!

Hunter's grabbed my wrist, and stuck his thumb in somewhere that really fuckin' hurts. 'Shut your mouth.'

'Come on, Craig. It's at least ten inch—AAAGH!'

Shite, something fuckin' snapped in there.

'Stop it!' Big meaty fists push us away, backwards until I fall.

Hunter's grip yanks me upright. Christ, the big bastard is so strong that he can lift me like a child. All fourteen stone. Bloody hell.

'Craig, back off.' Shepherd's between us, pushing Hunter away. Not many men have that kind of strength.

'You hear what he—'

'Sticks and stones, Craig. Sticks and stones.'

Something passes over Hunter's eyes. Something I don't like, frankly.

I'm in for it. Maybe not now, but soon.

Well, bring it on.

Shepherd grabs my sleeve and hauls us away from them and my fresh beer. 'What's going on?'

He's not holding anything. 'You not drinking, Luke?'

'No, and it's not a crime.'

'You're not an alcoholic, are you?'

'What, like you?' Shepherd shakes his head at us. 'No, I'm driving. And you're not even a beer in and you're being a toxic wee shite. Not that you need alcohol for that.'

'You starting on us now?'

'Brian, I was watching that. You were clearly the instigator, winding Craig up until he snapped. I'm advising you, as a superior officer, to shut up and drink your beer, then bugger off.'

Cullen appears through the door, his hungry eyes are searching everywhere, being a right nosy bastard.

Angela Caldwell joins him, towering over him. And she's wearing flats too. Christ.

Time I check on Paula.

Shepherd doesn't notice me slip off, and I snatch my beer from behind Buxton, then walk over and plant myself between Eva and Paula.

Eva looks round at us. 'So Hunter's still got thin skin, then?'

'Aye, and then some. Last thing I need is to let myself get into another fight, especially in front of Cullen, Shepherd and Caldwell. I'll lose my pension, and I really need it.'

Paula sips from a glass of water. 'That's rich.'

'What is?'

'Well, her turning up like that and you saying that.'

She's so pished that it doesn't make *any* sense to anyone. Not me, not to Eva.

So I frown at her. 'Come again?'

Paula leans in close. 'Well, Angela the golden girl... Turns out, after her husband died, Cullen and Methven framed it so that she got a survivor's pension.'

I remember that. Big bugger too. Roid rage drove him potty. 'That's the truth?'

'Totally.'

I thought I had a loaded gun in my pocket, but she's just

handed us a nuclear weapon. 'Back in a sec.' I get up and go out into the corridor, phone's out and dialling by the time I cross the threshold.

I try calling Carolyn's personal moby again. And I'm bounced to voicemail. Christ!

So I try her office. Picked up straight away, and I jump in before her. 'Hi, Elaine, is she back?'

'Sorry, Brian, but she's really busy just now.'

'Tell her it's urgent. More urgent than before.'

'Will do. Have a good evening.' Click, and Elaine is gone. Doesn't sound like she's got the message, but you've got to trust, haven't you?

Don't know how, but I'm outside the station in the wind and rain. Feel a bit pished, to be honest.

And Hunter comes out, too, with that look in his eyes, like he's going to lamp us. I flinch, shut my eyes like a wee prick, but he walks past. There's a CCTV camera by the phone box, isn't there? And he's gone, away from us. I'm safe.

But there's an idea. The phone box. Probably more a tramp's toilet these days, but if I call Carolyn on it, she'll maybe answer an unknown number.

Christ, I've got a couple of pound coins too. I stick the first one in and tap in her number. Like going back in time this, but it might just work.

The door opens behind us.

'Just a minute, pal.' I can't look around, because some cunt's punched us in the kidneys.

I go down on my knees and the receiver cracks us on the fuckin' teeth. Another boot in the arse too. A knee in the back, and I try to elbow the cunt, but he's grabbing my wrist and smacking it off the glass.

Twice, three times, feels like it's fuckin' broken.

A boot in the back, and the cunt crunches us down on my ribs with his knee. Then again. Like he's fuckin' launching himself down.

Then it's like he's grabbing my hair, but fuck me I've not got any hair anymore so it's my fuckin' scalp he's got a hold of.

'You don't talk about other men's girlfriends. Okay?'

Hunter. Fuck sake.

'Craig, you can fuckin' do one.'

He smashes my head off the pavement and I have to shut my eyes. Another boot in the back and they reopen again.

I try to shout, try to plead with him to stop.

'You even mention her name again and I will fucking kill you. And they won't find your body.'

One final boot to the skull and my head fuckin' scones off the glass again, cracks it but doesn't shatter it.

I lie there, eyes clamped shut, and all I hear is footsteps walking away.

Then a small voice. 'Hello? Are you okay?'

Soutar returned my fuckin' call!

25

E ven masked up, Cullen could tell it was Apinya Bain standing there, arms folded over her A&E scrubs. 'You?'

'Aye, it's me.' Cullen adjusted his own mask and put his hands into his pockets. 'I know you're not my number one fan, but I just need to see DCI Methven.'

She still wouldn't make eye contact. 'Right. Brian was really hurt when you demoted him.'

'He went to America without approval for his annual leave. I had no choice.'

That looked like news to her.

'How is Methven?'

'Not good.' Apinya's cheeks puffed up, like she was smiling but maybe grimacing. 'I'm afraid I can't let you see him.'

'It's that bad?'

'He's in surgery.'

Shite.

Cullen had many, many uses for a time machine, but going back there to save Methven would be right at the top of his list now.

'Scott.'

Cullen swung around.

DCS Carolyn Soutar was clutching a coffee cup, her face

mask pulled low as she sucked through the lid. Her hair was salon-perfect, but God knows where she got that these days. 'Come with me.' She led him away from Apinya.

Cullen gave her a curt nod as he followed Soutar. 'She said he's in surgery?'

'Indeed.' Soutar sat in the waiting area reserved for families, but Mrs Methven wasn't there. The adjacent seats were blocked off for social distancing. 'It's not looking good for Colin.'

'Is he going to die?'

Soutar rested the coffee on the chair between them. 'I spoke to the surgeon's PA, who told me that Colin's broken his back in two places. As much as he thinks he is, he's not Batman, so he won't be returning from a broken back any time soon.'

It hit Cullen harder than the virus. Like he was being choked, just like Isobel Geddes had been. His feet locked tight, and felt like they were the only things keeping from him toppling over onto the floor.

'Are you okay?'

'No.' Cullen shut his eyes. He was really, really far from okay. 'I owe him a lot.'

'Colin is a great investigator, a great leader, and a very driven man. Almost as much as you are, Scott.' Sounded like she slurped more coffee. 'He's been useful for me too, and he has solved several problems, while only creating a few in return. Hopefully he can be useful in the future.'

Cullen reopened his eyes. She was staring right at him. He sat back. 'I want to stay here. Find out how he is.'

'That's very noble, Scott. Thing is, while DCI Methven is still in surgery, DC Bain is in here, too. In a very bad state, I hasten to add. I had to call an ambulance for him.'

Cullen caught a flash of it, Hunter's brutality, his punches and kicks and knee drops, all the moves Cullen wanted to have done himself to Bain over the years. All over some stupid knob joke. But he didn't see the hurt it caused. The deep pain.

Hunter was a good guy, a good cop, and he had issues. Who didn't? But Bain was a nasty piece of shit, the kind who knew how to probe Hunter's issues, and how to exploit them, and for no gain, no reason.

No wonder Hunter had just exploded.

And it wasn't an isolated thing. Bain had been a complete bastard for years. Getting away with shit, then clinging on to his position, then going from DI to DC.

'Scott, I gather he was assaulted in a phone box outside St Leonard's.'

'A phone box?'

'I'm surprised too. I thought they were all closed down, but no.' She sniffed. 'What happened?'

'I didn't see anything.'

'No?'

'Nope.'

'Because I heard it was DC Craig Hunter who hospitalised DC Bain.'

Shite. Cullen's felt a thick lump in the back of his throat. 'Who did you hear that from?'

Down the corridor, a hospital porter scraped the floor, whistling, headphone cable dangling down to his pocket.

Soutar looked at Cullen, that deep stare that showed she was on to him and she wanted him to know. 'You're good, Scott.'

'What?'

'Relax, Craig won't face any charges for this.'

'Did he do it, though?'

'I had DS Shepherd look into the CCTV and Hunter walked off in the other direction from the assault location, which was in a blind spot... The next CCTV picks Hunter up still walking away in the opposite direction ... Now if someone was fast on their feet, brutal with their fists and had knowledge that certain cameras were out, I suppose it was possible DC Hunter could have done it quickly and with military efficiency, then high-tailed it back to his route as if nothing happened, but the more likely answer is, someone else did it and DC Bain is blaming Hunter.'

That didn't sit right with Cullen.

Hunter had gone right over the score, and should face something.

'Even though Shepherd's with the Complaints?'

'He's not any more. Besides, he's one of my people. I can

trust Luke.' But her brushing it under the carpet felt like there was another shoe to drop. 'I've just spoken to Brian. As you know, Scott, we go way back.'

Cullen felt his heart thud hard, fast.

'One of my greatest regrets is keeping Bain on the force. He called in a few favours, and I went along with it, knowing he is capable of good work. Tonight, he tried to use something against you.'

'What?'

'DC Bain is a desperate man, who won't go down without a fight, and certainly not without taking others with him, and he decided to drop another bomb. He divulged some hearsay about ADS Caldwell's pension.'

The last thing Cullen needed. On top of it all. How he and Methven had colluded to protect her, financially. Now Methven was lying in A&E with a broken neck, Cullen was the last man standing. It was so stupid of them, thinking that they would get away with cheating.

Cullen took a deep breath. 'Ma'am, we—'

'Don't try to deny it, Scott. I know you did it. And you know who told me.'

'Bain?'

'No, Scott. You don't pull a trick like this without involving the boss. DCI Methven told me. And I rubber-stamped it.'

She was in as deep as they were.

'What's going to happen, ma'am?'

'I've spoken to the surgeon and it looks like Colin is going to be invalided out. He won't be able to serve again. He's going to take the full blame for any fallout, so we can manage it that way.'

'So Angela won't lose out?'

'After what her husband did, no, she's an innocent here.'

'And what about me?'

'I could demote you, Scott. I could put you back in uniform and let you rot.'

Cullen knew he'd deserve it. But it would stop him doing what he was best at. What he needed to do.

'But I'd rather not, Scott. You've been useful to me. So you can keep your position.'

The surge of relief was overpowering, but it was tinged by the fear of what else would come from his indiscretion.

'Trouble is, Scott, I need an adult around here to look after you. Colin's been useful, sure, but it's still way too much like the Wild West and I can't have that. As of tonight, DI Davenport is going to take over from Methven as Acting DCI.'

Ally Davenport. Right back to the start. Great.

'And what about DC Bain?'

'What about him?' She licked her lips. 'Forgot to say, DS Caldwell passed her exam. I got the results fast tracked. You might wish to pass on the good news.'

CULLEN PULLED up on the street. It had been a while since he had visited Garleton in the early evening, but the view down to the coast through Long Vennel was stunning, the Christmas lights on the dim street matching by the glow of Drem and Gullane this side of the water, and the dark Forth in the distance. He killed the ignition and let the engine die away. 'Better face the music.'

Angela sat back in the chair, arms folded. She didn't look like she was going anywhere. That half-hour drive back from Edinburgh hadn't been enough to force out whatever she needed to say, though. 'You've been quiet.'

'Sorry. Been one of those days. Forgot to say, you passed your exam, Sergeant.'

She looked over and her eyes were red. 'Seriously?'

'What's up? Thought you'd be happy?'

She flashed up her eyebrows. 'Paula knows about what you did for me. The pension.'

'Right. How does she know?'

'I've no idea. Will I lose it?'

'I'll do whatever I can to protect you, Angela.'

'But will that be enough?'

Cullen could only shrug. He didn't want to implicate Soutar in anything, but it was more like protecting Angela.

'Don't put yourself in danger for me, Scott.'

'People in senior positions have got your back too. But me and Methven made a decision, not you. We chose to do this because it was the right thing. You lost your husband, your kids lost their father. None of that was your fault. And I don't want you suffering for it.'

'Thank you, Scott.' She smiled at him, then brushed a tear away. 'Speaking of suffering.' She nodded over his shoulder.

Cullen swung round to see Evie charging down the path towards them, arms folded across her chest in that way that screamed out how much shite he was in.

Angela was already round that side of the car, hugging Evie and asking about her demonic sons. She looked over at the house. 'Where are they?'

'Little one's sleeping and Dec's playing that Switch thing.'

'Good.'

Cullen got out onto the street. 'How was it?'

'It was good.' Evie wrapped him in a hug and whispered, 'It confirmed that I never want kids.'

Angela rolled her eyes. 'I was going to ask if you wanted mine.'

EPILOGUE

Two months later

I use the wee dial thing to swivel around and take another long look around the place, but it's got a bit of a delay. I mean, I'm up here in the far north and that pub of mine, The Cheeky Judge, is doing a roaring trade. Doors open to the public, inside without even masks on. Spent many a drunken hour in here. Place has potential, that's for sure. Shifted the bar over to the far wall, got some taps in straight to the kegs. Stuck in some more tables and stools. Still cops mostly drinking in here, and they're different these days, so I've put on food and coffees.

Aye, it has a lot of promise.

And good old Alan Irvine is behind the bar. Nice to get the grant money for employing a man who'd paid his debt to society, isn't it? An ex-jailbird, maybe, but an ex-copper, and one who the regulars love.

'The Cheeky Judge, eh?' I give a sly look to the four faces in Zoom. 'Never met a judge who wasn't just the straightest and most boring twat, ever, but hey ho.'

Big Malky McKeown is top left. Brains behind this. Well, the technical side, eh? 'Why did you keep the name?'

'Oh, the name needed to endure, believe me. Has done for a

long time. I bought that place, but it's not just bricks and mortar, it's a brand.'

Can't smell it, mind, but the place still reeks of pish and mould, mind. That takes a lot of cleaning.

Willie is supposed to be top right, stupid fud is struggling to work his phone, so he's got it on camera not selfie view, so the rest of us just across Applecross Bay. I mean... 'So, are you serious, Brian?'

'Aye, I'm deadly serious. I got stitched up, didn't I? Booted off the force, no pension. Got the shite kicked out of us.' I point up at the wounds that still bloody ache. 'I mean, can you credit it?'

'If Scott Cullen's involved, I can believe anything.' Willie's face fills up his window, and the old sod's scowling like a sex case. 'Way you told me it, though, Soutar sacked you.'

'Aye, but I've had a wee chat with her. She's blaming Sundance for what happened to Crystal Methven and to me. Bottom line, Cullen's going down. Him and Hunter.'

'But you'll need help?'

'And I've got help.'

'Eh?'

'Willie, the two people you don't know on this bloody call!'

The bottom two faces are those two fannies, masks on like they're cooking up crystal meth in that show on telly, but they're in the *Argus*'s newsroom. Richard McAlpine and Alan Lyall.

'Boys.' Can't help myself but wink at them. 'Tell you, Willie, the stories we're going to get off the boys and girls in this boozer? It's all going to be used to fuck over Scott Cullen.'

I look back up at the pub screen on my telly and there she is. Wee Eva, working a treat as she chats to Buxton and Hunter at the back of the room. Gave them a bottomless tab, and the stupid buggers have been firing in for three hours. And they're on strong stuff.

I flick off the mute, and Hunter's speaking. 'Aye, I mean, it doesn't matter where you're fighting, really, but a phone box gives you an advantage if you attack first.'

Bingo.

Loose lips sink ships.
And they'll nail Scott Cullen and Craig Hunter to the wall!

SCOTT CULLEN WILL RETURN

CULLEN 9

WILL IT HAVE A NAME?

WILL IT BE OUT IN 2021?

WHO CAN SAY?

Before that comes, I will publish "DEAD IN THE WATER", a prequel short novel showing how Cullen met Bain, but also featuring Craig Hunter and some of the rest of the gang.

If you want to receive it free three months before it hits Amazon, and would like to be kept up to date with new releases from Ed James, please join my Readers' Club.

OTHER BOOKS BY ED JAMES

SCOTT CULLEN MYSTERIES SERIES

1. GHOST IN THE MACHINE
2. DEVIL IN THE DETAIL
3. FIRE IN THE BLOOD
4. STAB IN THE DARK
5. COPS & ROBBERS
6. LIARS & THIEVES
7. COWBOYS & INDIANS
8. HEROES & VILLAINS

CULLEN & BAIN SERIES

1. CITY OF THE DEAD
2. WORLD'S END
3. HELL'S KITCHEN
4. GORE GLEN

CRAIG HUNTER SERIES

1. MISSING
2. HUNTED
3. THE BLACK ISLE

DS VICKY DODDS

1. TOOTH & CLAW
2. FLESH & BLOOD
3. SKIN & BONE (May 2021)

DI SIMON FENCHURCH SERIES

1. THE HOPE THAT KILLS

CORCORAN & PALMER

Made in the USA
Las Vegas, NV
30 January 2021